LOVE HERTZ

AARON MOSTOW
KEVIN FLORES
RODOLFO TAGLE III

Published by

LOVE HERTZ, LLC

Los Angeles, California

This is a work of fiction. Unless otherwise indicated, all the names, characters, businesses, places, events and incidents in this book are either the product of the authors' imagination or used in a fictitious manner.

ISBN: 978-0-578-94691-7

LOVE HERTZ

CHAPTER ONE

TAKE A LAP

Taj tried for a casual gait, but he crossed the floor too fast. Not a single head turned his way except the bearded bartender who watched him, unimpressed. Taj's credit card was draining away at the table with his friends, so he gave the bartender an awkward nod and turned around. Everyone knew the best players took a lap before settling down.

"Slower. Like I own the place. I could have any woman here," Taj encouraged himself.

It didn't help the knotted-up worry in his gut that no woman actually did look his way, that he would die a revirginized store clerk, but it did make him try harder.

Taj added a smile at a passing woman, but it only served to confuse her. She sidestepped him as she waved at a tall man leaning on the bar. Taj appreciated the bounce of her breasts and wondered if the man's bored scowl was the secret to exciting women.

"What are you scowling about?" Taj's rotund friend bumped into him.

"Just taking a lap, Phatty, checking for talent," Taj said. He adjusted the cuffs on his button-down shirt and then smoothed back his black hair.

"Well, you should check out the chicks that Skyler just brought back to the table." Phatty pointed across the lounge with his chin while precariously balancing the cheese plate in his hands.

Taj headed back and made it to the table just in time to see the blonde toss her hair. She didn't let his exuberant landing in the seat next to her stop the story she was being begged to tell.

"So, like, I gave him my number and he ends up coming over to my place for dinner the next night," she said.

Taj caught her gesticulating hand and shook it. "Hi, I'm Taj."

"Nicky." Her nose crinkled up as she yanked her hand free.

"Well, go on," Skyler D said.

Skyler D leaned back and looped one arm around Nicky's friend. He rubbed the shoulder of her sequin dress until she shifted in her seat, tucked her body against him, and rested her hand on his thigh. Skyler D parted his legs farther and gave Taj an eyebrow waggle.

"Where was I?" Nicky leaned as far away from Taj as possible and then continued her story.

"Oh yeah, so he comes over and asks if he can help make dinner. I'm just making spaghetti, whatever, but he comes up behind me in the kitchen."

"And then what?" Phatty made it to the table and dropped

the remaining cheese squares in the middle of the tablecloth.

Nicky savored the attention with a smile. "Then he flips my skirt up, kneels down and starts licking my ass. I was like, O-M-G ! But it was the best feeling ever."

Even Skyler D's jaw dropped.

Taj took his opportunity. "So, what are you doing later? Can I have your number?"

Nicky turned blank eyes on Taj. "Huh?"

He fumbled for his phone and tried to toss it to her. It clattered onto the now empty cheese plate and knocked over two beer bottles.

Skyler D jumped up and Nicky's friend almost tumbled to the floor. She caught herself on the tablecloth but spilled the rest of her wine.

The music briefly stopped as he repeated the question. "I said, can I have your number?"

Taj's question left an awkward silence. The music resumed as Nicky stood up and rolled her eyes. "Um, like, how 'bout I just get yours?" she said as she pulled out her phone.

"Great!" Taj rattled off his number, then dove for his phone before an irritated waitress cleared the table.

Nicky pretended to take his number and left the table in a hurry.

When Taj turned around, everyone was weaving toward the door without him.

Taj caught up to his friends and climbed in the back seat of Skyler D's car. He was feeling pretty good about himself, remembering any small success he'd had at the lounge that night: the confused smile he'd gotten from a passing woman, the surprised double-take the waitress did when he asked how her night was and flirtations his friends hadn't even seen.

Then Skyler D saw him in the rearview mirror.

"Can I have your number?" Skyler D did a high-pitch impression of Taj's voice. He shook his head and laughed. "Damn, Taj, what the hell were you thinking?"

"Dude, what's that supposed to mean?" Taj asked.

Skyler D checked his sandy-brown hair in the rearview mirror. It was still perfect. "You have absolutely no game, bro."

Taj slumped back in the car seat and crossed his arms over his chest. "She was into me."

Skyler D snorted in disbelief.

Taj grabbed both headrests and heaved himself forward. "Dude, she was really into me! She was totally playing footsies with me under the table."

Phatty stopped gazing at a passing Taco Bell and frowned at Taj. "Wait, what?"

"I'm telling you guys, she was rubbing her foot all up and down my leg."

"That was my foot, you idiot!" Phatty said.

Taj started to protest, but his shoulders slumped. "I thought it was kinda big for a girl. Gross."

"Ha! Taj, you couldn't get laid even if you were landing in Hawaii with a hula girl sitting on your face," Skyler D said.

"Fuck you." Taj slumped back again.

Phatty forgot about his foot seducing Taj under the table when he checked his phone. "Yo, there's an afterhours right up the street. Let's go!"

"I'm down," Skyler D said. "Let's see what's poppin'."

"Nah, not me." Taj lifted his chin. "I've gotta go home and wait for Nicky's call."

He was glad only the front door light was on when he got home. Taj's family was asleep. He closed the car door quietly, then winced as Skyler D backed out of the driveway honking and laughing.

Taj crept into the house and upstairs to his room. He was tired, but laughter and pulsing house music still rang in his ears. He sat down at his desk and waited for the quiet of the suburbs to sink in. Then he took out his phone and carefully laid it on top of his synthesizer keyboard.

"She's gonna call," he told himself, but his words sounded hollow in the quiet. "Why don't they ever call?"

CHAPTER TWO

DJ SPELLS DAY JOB

Taj groaned as the rhythmic music of his alarm got louder. In his dreams he was on stage, facing a bouncing crowd of adoring women. The music got louder, and he scanned the fantasy crowd.

The women's faces were blurry, and Taj knew deep down they weren't really looking at him. No matter how hard he tried, the opposite sex didn't see anything but a scrawny young man with thick black hair and an awkward smile. His Macaulay Culkin-esque boyish features didn't exactly scream sex symbol, often leaving him home alone.

Reality yanked him out of the dream.

He untangled himself from the twin sheets of his bed and sat up. With one eye cracked open, he stopped the insistent alarm.

"The beats were all wrong. That's all," Taj told himself.

He sat for a minute and wondered what track would give him a better dream.

Then he scrubbed both eyes and excitedly opened his call history.

It was blank.

"Ah, man. She didn't even call." Taj tossed his phone back on his desk.

Only a few feet separated his bed from the bathroom, but Taj walked as if it were death row. The guys had known that Nicky wouldn't call, but no one could tell him why.

Taj felt better after washing his face. With a fresh expression, he straightened his thin shoulders and practiced flirty smiles in the mirror. He marched back into his room and was delighted to find a new message on his computer.

He sat down at his desk, flexed his fingers and opened the dating website. Taj read out loud: "Hi, I'm Bonnie. Read your profile and you sound sexy. Can't wait to find out about your many talents."

Bonnie's profile was incomplete, but Taj studied the few photographs carefully. After a few minutes of tracing all her curves with his eyes, he decided she was hot. Even Skyler D would think she was a hottie.

"And she wants to know about my talents." Taj chuckled.

He pushed away from his desk and fought the urge to dance around the room.

He settled for a few satisfied head nods to congratulate himself.

"I knew the platinum membership would pay off!"

Even an abrupt knock on the door couldn't knock the smile off Taj's face. He jumped up and grabbed a bottle of lotion and box of tissues off the nightstand.

"My nights with you are over!" Taj tossed them under the bed and went to his bedroom door. "Who is it?"

"It's your father," a gruff voice told him.

"Yeah, what's up, Dad?"

Prasad opened his son's door and cautiously stepped into the room. He looked around at the scattered mess and sighed.

He spied Bonnie's profile still open on Taj's computer.

"What's this now? Another waste of money?"

Taj closed the tab and uncovered his latest project.

Prasad gave him a stern look. "Are you still making those fucking beats? My god, you should be an engineer like your brother by now."

"What do you want, Dad?" Taj rolled his eyes and turned the volume up on his computer.

His father ground his teeth. "You're supposed to open up the liquor store today."

"I know, Dad. But, listen. I'm really onto something with this new beat. It's gonna be a hit. I'm DJing at the Pearl tonight and I'm gonna drop it in my set." Taj reached for the volume again.

Prasad slapped Taj's hand. "A waste of your college education."

"Just listen—"

"You call this music?" Prasad glared at his son.

Taj felt his father's disgust like a rock pressing hard against his chest. It was hard to breathe, much less explain the way he felt about making music. And it wasn't like he hadn't tried before. The morning was starting to feel like every other day, with his father prodding him in one direction while Taj's heart was leading him the other way.

"Dad, music is my passion. This music. It's what I love.

Why can't you understand that?" Taj's voice rose in frustration.

"What you love isn't making you money. I can't understand how you don't see that. You need to start thinking about your future, Taj."

Taj gritted his teeth in an expression that mirrored his father's irritation. "We've talked about this a thousand times. This is my future."

Prasad took a step toward his stubborn son. "I'll tell you about your future. You'll be living off your mother's leftovers and sleeping on your friends' secondhand couches. No bed of your own. No computer. No little music toys."

Taj slid over instinctively to protect his synthesizer keyboard. "Whatever, Dad."

"Don't 'whatever' me, Taj! I'm giving you a year to get your act together or else you're out of here." Prasad crossed his arms over his chest. "You will no longer live in my house and I will no longer support you financially."

Taj's mouth dropped open.

"No way. You wouldn't."

"Why wouldn't I? I've worked hard for everything I have, and I don't need a financial burden," Prasad said.

"A burden? Does Mom know you're up here saying this?" Taj asked.

Prasad's face darkened. "I'm giving you a year."

Taj dropped down onto his twin bed. He knew he shouldn't have dragged his mother into the conversation. She had enough worries as it was.

"A year? Fine. This is my life, not yours," Taj muttered.

"And what kind of life is it?" Prasad asked. He gestured around Taj's messy childhood room. "You hang out with your friends, listen to that ridiculous music and chase women not even worthy of your time. Is this really what you want?"

Taj punched the bed. "You don't care about what I want."

"Because I want you to grow up, Taj."

"Whatever, Dad."

Prasad threw his hands up. "I give you everything and all I get is 'whatever.'

"Your bad attitude doesn't change the fact that as long as you live in my house you will obey my rules. And starting next week, I don't want to hear this bullshit in my house anymore."

"Fine." Taj stood up and showed his father the door. "If that's what you really want, I'll be outta here in a year."

"Good." Prasad marched into the hall. "Now get your ass to the store!"

Taj took his time opening the liquor store. It had been one of his father's first wise investments, and he never failed to remind Taj he bought the tight little storefront right out of college. To his father, the liquor store represented hard work, ownership and a secure future.

"Someone always wants liquor," Taj imitated his father. "Man, do I know how that someone feels."

To Taj, the liquor store represented breaking his back hefting cases of beer. It was hours spent sweeping up broken glass and mopping up the pungent fumes of different boozes.

And it was long stretches standing behind the cash register watching the world pass him by.

Taj hated seeing all the dressed-up people on their way to dinners, parties and dates.

"Come on, Bonnie. Respond. I could totally bring over a good wine." Taj checked his phone again. He'd crafted a long and sensuous message to the girl on the dating website, but she wasn't writing back.

Taj then checked his social media and shook his head. Why hadn't anyone liked his selfies with expensive booze? With the right filters and editing, he could block out the bright, fluorescent lights of the liquor store and make it seem like he was a rich party animal.

"Maybe something's wrong with my profile or something." Taj nodded at an incoming customer and then concentrated on his profile.

He had two followers: his mom and DJ Phatty.

At least Phatty's feed cheered Taj up. His friend lived in a house jam-packed with sisters and one was always photobombing or pranking him.

Taj switched back to his profile. Much cooler, he decided with a nod. The customer approached Taj at the register and plunked a six-pack of beer on the counter. "And some cigarettes too," the man said.

"Sure." Taj turned around.

"Yeah, those. The yellow pack."

With Taj's back turned, the customer saw his phone on the counter and grabbed it to take a closer look. The man chuckled. "Is this you? That's some image you're selling."

Taj snatched his phone back, rang the man up and flipped him off as he walked out the door.

"What do you know? I am selling an image: the best DJ around. I am the party."

That was his only customer for nearly an hour. Finally,

Taj gave up watching his deserted social media accounts. Bonnie never messaged him back. He pocketed his phone and headed over to the magazine rack.

"Maybe I need a sexy career. Something women really love." Taj grabbed a copy of *Popular Mechanics* but was bored by the fourth page. He tossed it back and grabbed a new DJ magazine. "Seriously, what does my dad know? DJing is the sexiest and best career out there."

Hours dragged on at work as Taj's anticipation built for his debut DJ performance.

A good-looking couple holding hands walked in as Taj was talking to himself. He greeted them and then scooted back to the counter as quick as he could. The DJ magazine remained unopened as he watched the couple on the security monitors.

The man tugged her close and whispered in her ear something that made her smile and lean closer. They strolled contentedly up and down the aisles, snuggling and comparing labels.

"Is there anything I can help you find?" Taj called out.

"Nah, we're fine," the man said. He kissed his girlfriend on the cheek.

They bought two bottles of wine and walked out of the store still holding hands.

Taj was still gazing after them when two girls in miniskirts and high heels came tripping in the door.

"So, I was like, no, Brian. That's not happening," the taller one said.

"Ugh, Brian? Why would anyone date him?" She scowled as she fluffed up her curly hair.

"Sup, ladies. I'm not Brian," Taj called out. He leaned on the counter and gave them both a sexy smile.

The taller one rolled her eyes. The other one sighed and said, "Um, gross."

"So, what do you want to drink?" The taller one tugged her friend down the nearest aisle. "And no. We don't need help finding anything."

"Um, I like Corona." The other girl fluffed up her curls again.

"Okay." The tall one reached down to grab a twelve-pack of Corona. Her short skirt slipped up and up.

Taj leaned farther over the counter. As the girl tugged on the case of beer, her skirt flapped higher. He could see the rounded curves of both butt cheeks and a small strip of neon pink satin.

"Now those are major assets!" Taj quickly checked his hair in the reflective background of a beer sign.

The girls shoved the twelve-pack of Corona onto the counter, unaware of why Taj's smile was so heated.

"That'll be $18.68, please," he said. Then his eyes trailed past the girl's fluffy curls and dipped down into her cleavage. She swiped her card and glared at him when he finally looked up.

"Here's your receipt," Taj said. He then yanked a flyer out of his back pocket. "Hey, check it out. I'm DJing tonight at the Pearl. Come over, I'll put you on the list!"

The taller one rolled her eyes again but took the flyer. "Thanks."

"Yeah, no problem. Try to get there early, it's gonna be a packed house!"

The girls teetered out the door on their high heels and didn't look back. Halfway across the parking lot the taller one dug in her pocket for her keys and pulled out the flyer again.

"What a creeper," she told her friend.

"Yeah, I know. He probably sucks at DJing," said the curly-haired one.

"He probably can't even make a cobra dance."

They both laughed. Then she dropped the flyer. It fluttered to the ground and stuck to the edge of a small puddle, soaking up the muddy water. The girls got into a white S-Class Mercedes and drove away.

Inside, Taj whistled through the rest of his work, even sweeping with extra energy. He counted the money, imagined making three times that for one gig and turned off the neon "open" sign. He locked the liquor store door and smiled to himself in the reflection.

"Looking good tonight, Taj," he told himself.

Halfway to his car, Taj noticed the smeared flyer stuck to the ground. He frowned, looked around and slumped his shoulders.

"Maaaaaaan. Oh well. One day I'll be the best DJ out there and girls will be chasing me." He forced a smile and was back to whistling by the time he reached his car.

CHAPTER THREE

A TOTAL CROC

It took two tries before the beaten-up door of Taj's old Honda Civic would close. He bumped it with his hip just to make sure. Someday soon he was going to trade in the little economy beater for a Maserati. Or maybe a Bentley.

If everything went the way Taj imagined it, this was the night that would rocket him toward fame and wealth.

Or he'd end up living in that rusty little car by the end of the year.

Taj walked faster to escape that thought. Everything was in front of him: the Pearl, his friends and his best chance to make it as a DJ. He shuffled across the parking lot in his lucky shoes with his laptop tucked safely under his arm.

The bouncer stopped Taj on sight and shook his head.

"No, man, go home."

"I'm the DJ!" Taj pointed at the crumpled flyer stapled to the entry wall.

The burly man blocked the door and took in Taj's outfit: a tight yellow polo shirt, cargo shorts, white tube socks and green Crocs.

"I keep telling management there should be a dress code," he muttered.

The bouncer looked him up and down again and kept shaking his head, even when he found Taj's name on the list. Taj thanked him and slipped into the nightclub. It took a minute for his eyes to adjust to the pulsating light. The high-energy music bombarded him, and Taj wandered through the crowd momentarily stunned. The fog machines made him cough, and he squinted at every knot of people he passed.

"What the fuck are you wearing, bro?"

Taj squinted and coughed. "What's up, Skyler?"

"Seriously, man. What the fuck are you wearing?" Skyler asked again.

"My good-luck Crocs," Taj said. He lifted up one tube-socked leg to show his friend. "My feet get really sweaty when I'm nervous."

"Whoa! No! Put that thing down. I don't want to smell your sweaty feet." Skyler backed off and glanced around, hoping no one was looking. A few girls giggled, but they smiled shyly at Skyler.

"You sure those Crocs are lucky?" Skyler asked. "I mean, they haven't really panned out for you at nightclubs before."

"Trust me." Taj grinned and slapped his friend on the back.

Skyler groaned and his bleach-white teeth glowed brightly under the blacklight. He was wearing sunglasses against the flickering glare of the club's light show.

They also hid the pitying expression Skyler gave his friend.

"Alright , man. Let's hope they really are good luck." Skyler spun Taj toward the stage. "This is your chance, so don't fuck it up. It's not just your reputation on the line!"

Taj, still dazed by the lights, wandered off course and had to be dragged back out of the crowd. Skyler's good looks and reputation as a hot local DJ kept people back a step or two, but Taj was bumped and trampled by everyone around him.

Skyler got him safely to a table near the side of the stage. "You're on in five minutes!"

"Thanks again, dude," Taj said. He scanned the crowd and spotted Phatty working his way toward them with two beers.

Skyler smacked Taj on the shoulder and pointed to his flashy watch. "Five minutes."

Skyler and Phatty exchanged looks as they passed each other. Phatty shrugged it off and handed Taj one of the beers.

"You going on right now?" Phatty asked over the thumping house music.

"Yup!"

"Awesome." Phatty held out his beer bottle in a quick toast. Then he tipped back the beer and chugged it down. "Ahh, that's good."

Taj laughed as Phatty's belch rivaled the bass of the music. His friend didn't care that a passing pair of girls gave him a disgusted look. Phatty was out of the house and away from his sisters; it was time to have fun.

"Okay, see you in a little," Taj said.

"Cool, man. Rock it up there!" Phatty took Taj's half-full beer and finished it for him.

The music stopped as Taj climbed the narrow side steps up to the stage curtain. Skyler D, now sporting a designer sports coat, strolled out on stage and caught the crowd's attention.

"Alright, party people! You know me, Skyler D!" The crowd cheered. "Well, tonight I've got something new for you. Making his Pearl debut, give it up for Taj!"

Taj stumbled out from behind the curtain and squinted under the bright lights. The crowd didn't cheer like they had for Skyler—instead they paused.

Some were pointing at Taj's outfit and more than a dozen phones were out instantly. He decided it was a compliment and waved as he plugged in his laptop.

Nerves shook his fingertips as he started to play and he accidentally pressed a large gray button on the DJ mixer.

The music stopped, causing the energetic movement of the stage lights to come to a halt.

Everyone in the club turned to glare at Taj.

Skyler D stood behind the curtain and closed his eyes. Then he lifted one eyelid and looked around, certain this was going to destroy his credibility.

He watched in despair as Taj panicked and pressed a dozen buttons in a frantic attempt to get the music started again.

Finally he hit the large gray button again and the music pumped out of the speakers.

But it was too late. Most of the people in the club were ignoring Taj completely. A few girls left the dance floor and headed to the bar. Then a few more. The opinionated exodus spread, and finally the only one anywhere near the stage was Phatty.

"Fuck, I knew it," Skyler D groaned.

There was another pause in the music and Skyler heard Phatty belch before saying, "Oh, no."

Taj finished the set, though by the end even he wasn't bouncing to the beats. He heard no applause, even after he picked up his laptop and left the stage. Skyler announced another DJ and the crowd slowly returned from the bar.

Taj had to shove his way through the clubbers to get back to Phatty's table. Luckily there was a drink already waiting for him.

"I don't know what happened," Taj told Phatty.

Before his sympathetic friend could answer, Skyler strode up to the table.

"That shit was weak, bro. No one was feeling it!" Skyler said. "I'm gonna be honest with you, man, you gotta drop beats that the chicks are gonna like. And change your clothes; that outfit is ridiculous. You're going to have to do a one-eighty to even have a chance to make it as a DJ, bro."

Taj furrowed his brow and looked down at his outfit. "You really think it would make a difference?"

Skyler took off his sunglasses and waved them in Taj's face. "You know how many gigs I've landed with these shades?"

"You do look kinda goofy, Taj," Phatty interjected.

"I guess my Crocs aren't as lucky as I thought," Taj said. He frowned down at his favorite shoes.

"You gotta do better than this, bro!" Skyler told him.

"You're right, dude. I got a lot of work to do." Taj finished his drink, tucked his laptop under his arm and headed for the door with his spirit in shambles.

Taj cringed under every streetlight as he drove home to his house in the suburbs. His first big break had been a huge disaster and even his friends were embarrassed. Not a single woman in the club had looked at Taj after his beats started.

"You gotta drop beats that chicks are gonna like..." Skyler D's voice echoed in Taj's mind as he turned down his street and headed home. His hands felt like lead on the steering wheel. For a moment, Taj imagined the circle of the wheel was an album.

The blurry garden lights on his neighbor's front lawn became the flashing strobes of a bursting new club. Taj felt the crowd pulsing in front of him.

Then a car honked behind him.

Taj waved an apology. He crawled through the stop sign and idled home. In the driveway, he turned off his car and sat in silence as long as he could stand.

Seconds later, Taj asked himself: "How am I supposed to do a one-eighty like Skyler said if I still always end up here?"

The claustrophobic air of the little economy car didn't have an answer. Neither did his blank phone or his unanswered social media. Maybe no one even noticed his colossal failure as a DJ.

Taj trudged inside and crept up to his bedroom. He viciously kicked his Crocs across the room and flopped down in his desk chair.

He switched on his purple mood lighting, plugged in his laptop and opened it up. The bright screen made Taj cringe. He turned the brightness down and started creating a new electronic dance beat.

It took off, and Taj plugged in his synthesizer keyboard.

He pulled on his headphones and it all came back to him: the imagined crowd pulsing up and down, the women screaming and the lights shining brightly down on him. Taj pictured his smiling face on a big screen, making all the women shriek even louder, their dancing hips gyrating and bumping.

The inspiration lasted far into the night until Taj fell asleep. His head dipped down onto his keyboard as he smiled and drooled. In his head, he dreamed up the best gimmicks; far better than Skyler D's boring sunglasses.

A heavy beat bumped against Taj's forehead, and, in his dream, he wrapped a long silk scarf around it. He turned into an odd hybrid of Mick Jagger, Axel Rose and a snake charmer. Not mysterious enough for electronic music. Taj needed something no one had seen before.

Better keep it simple and modern. Definitely a cat helmet and a suit. Taj's subconscious decided the logical color suit for a cat to wear was bronze, made from some shiny, itchy material.

Why did it itch? Wasn't this a dream?

Taj shifted his head over the keyboard and the beat changed. A new frequency was triggered, some sort of combination of where his nose and his eyebrow hit the keyboard while his forehead shifted knobs above the keys.

It moved in heavy waves and affected Taj's whole brain. And his whole dream.

Now he wore a wig, a green bandana and neon Spandex. If Taj thought the cat suit was itchy, his subconscious was unprepared for the leotard nightmare it had produced. His dream rode up and chafed, and he was so busy adjusting the Spandex that his fingers never touched the DJ equipment.

A snort of frustration turned into a snore and Taj turned his head on the keyboard again.

His dream view was blurred by thick reading glasses and Taj felt a distinct breeze on his head. It didn't match the ebb and flow of the new beats in his head. Taj reached up and felt his stubbled head. He grabbed a dream mirror, almost the exact replica of the reflective beer sign he used at work, and saw that half his head was shaved. And he was wearing all black, of course.

The mix of beats and the buzzing frequency was almost enough to rouse Taj from his dream. His desk chair creaked as he squirmed about, imagining that his dance moves stopped every female within a fifty-foot radius.

If only he had some magic talent, some secret weapon that made all women want him.

The dream twisted on Taj and he now appeared in the liquor store's glass door wearing traditional Indian wedding attire. His father stood behind him, his chest puffed out proudly, but his puckered look of disapproval still firmly in place.

Taj wanted to turn up the volume and drown out whatever his dream dad might say.

He struggled in his sleep and felt the beat intensify. They wove a new dream into Taj's subconscious, and he floated for a long time in an epic version of his favorite fantasy: world-renowned DJ, epic panty-dropper and rich enough to buy a hundred of his father's little liquor stores.

CHAPTER FOUR

WHAT IS THE FREQUENCY?

Taj pried his head off his keyboard at what he thought was a reasonable hour. He wiped the side of his mouth and then frowned at his laptop. There were creases on his face from the keys. In a panic, he jumped up. What time was it? Late. Much later than he thought.

"No! I look like a freak who escaped from a circus or something," he muttered.

He tried to slick his unruly hair down, but he stopped halfway through the tangles. Taj sat back down in his desk chair. As he came to his senses, he realized there was a faint sound in his room.

"What's that sound?" he wondered aloud.

An unusual frequency emanated from his speakers, which had unknowingly been recording all night.

Taj fiddled with one cut, changing the volume and some of the other settings, then got it so screwed up he had to revert back to the original.

He hummed along and leaned forward. He rested one cheek on his knuckles as he listened intently, then he went scrambling around the room. He snatched up and rejected four shirts and two pairs of pants before he pulled himself together. Then he sprinted to the bathroom and scrubbed his face with ice-cold water until the creases from his keyboard were no longer visible.

Taj walked downstairs at a casual pace and shuffled into the dining room as if he'd just woken up. He even faked a yawn and scratched at his hastily brushed hair.

"Good morning," he said to his family.

"It was. A few hours ago," his father said.

Taj's brother checked his phone, laughed at something and showed it to his gorgeous fiancé. Michelle covered her nearly perfect smile with one demure hand, but her well-rounded chest bounced with repressed laughter.

"What's so funny? Another job offer?" Prasad asked. "Taj! Did you know Mani has multiple job offers? Your brother is in such a good position now, he can afford to be picky."

"Yeah, I see that," Taj said as he stared at Michelle's chest.

"Taj!" his father barked. "Pass the curry."

Taj dragged his eyes off Michelle's cleavage and passed the curry as he'd been ordered. Prasad glared at his youngest son and then turned to Mani with a beaming smile.

"Mani, my son. You know it's always nice having you and Michelle here," Prasad said.

"Well, we love visiting you guys." Mani checked his phone again. Then his smug eyes flickered over to his younger brother. "So, Taj, how did the big show go last night?"

Taj swallowed hard. "Meh. It was alright, I guess."

He sat up a little taller and tried to smile when his mother walked into the room, but Taj's father wasn't done with him yet. Aashi gave her youngest son a loving smile and searched for a spot on the table to place down the rice bowl she had carried in.

Prasad grunted instead of saying thank you to his wife and then turned on his lecturing tone. "I told you, Taj, you should get a real career like your brother and make something of yourself. Stop wasting your time making those drops or beats or whatever you call them. Once you become an engineer, you'll find a beautiful woman like Michelle."

Aashi smacked her husband on the shoulder as he beamed at his soon-to-be daughter-in-law.

"Prasad, you leave your son alone. I like Taj's music."

His mother did a little dance, but Taj just hung his head. Across the table, Michelle fed a tantalizing bite to Mani.

He devoured it and they both smiled. It turned into a gaze, and Taj wished he could melt into the floor. Especially when Michelle caressed his brother's cheek and blinded Taj with the megawattage of her engagement ring.

Taj cleared his throat. "I'm not wasting my time, Dad. You'll see, just wait. I'm going to be a famous DJ one day. I'll be able to get any girl I want."

Prasad gave a mean laugh and turned to praise his eldest son some more. Taj dug into his food and suddenly understood why his friend Phatty liked to snack so much. It was a good way to keep his head down and not get dragged into any conversations.

Aashi sat down and patted Taj's hand. "So, Taj. Did you meet any beautiful women last night?"

Taj thought about all the women that had wandered off the dance floor during his set. They'd been so far away from him Taj hadn't really seen anyone.

When the embarrassing memory faded and his eyes came back into focus, Taj was staring directly at Michelle's cleavage again.

"You wish," Michelle mouthed disdainfully across the table before Taj dragged his eyes off her.

"Taj?" Aashi studied her youngest son's face with sweet concern.

"No, Mom, I didn't," Taj finally said.

Aashi patted his hand again and sighed.

The comforting sound turned into an aggressive cough. Aashi clutched Taj's hand and Prasad leaned over to put a comforting hand on his wife's back. She struggled and finally gained control of the cough.

Taj handed her a glass of water. "It sounds like your cough is getting worse."

Aashi gave him a pained look, worse than the cough that had just racked her small frame. "It's not for you to worry about, Taj. I just have to go back to the doctor for another checkup next week."

Mani cleared his throat. "You'll be fine, Mom. You're going to the best doctor in town. We're going to get through this."

Aashi gave everyone a brave smile. It turned Taj's stomach to see her look so drained.

"Can I be excused?" Taj asked.

"You may," Prasad responded.

Taj cleared the empty plates for his mother and carried them into the kitchen. He set them gently in the sink and began rinsing them. It took a minute before he was able to pick up the sponge and start scrubbing.

"Taj," Aashi said, walking into the kitchen.

Taj glanced over his shoulder and gave his mother a half-hearted smile. Then he went back to scrubbing, glad for the distraction.

"You know, your dad just wants what's best for you," she continued.

He flicked the soapsuds off his hands and frowned at the mention of his father. Aashi crossed the kitchen and laid a hand on her son's cheek.

Taj's face softened.

"I know, Mom. You keep telling me that."

Aashi smiled. Then she looped her hand around Taj's shoulder and pulled him closer. "But no matter what, let your instincts guide you. Always do what you love, Taj. Always."

Taj blinked back tears but smiled. "Thanks, Mom. That's what I needed to hear."

He hugged her and then hurried out of the kitchen and back up to his bedroom.

That strange sound had been in his head all through the family meal and Taj was anxious to hear it again. His instincts told him that sound was something special and he was determined to figure out why.

Taj flopped onto his desk chair and flipped open his laptop. The sound started again and his eyes lit up. It was a strange combination that felt like it resonated through his bones.

"Some kind of buzzing? Did I bust a speaker?" Taj wondered aloud.

He picked up his laptop and checked all around. There wasn't a scratch on it despite Skyler D using it for a drink coaster at the club. He checked his speaker wiring and all the connections. Nothing looked out of the ordinary. Taj closed everything except his mixer. Then he started to review what he had recorded the night before.

He searched until he found a particular-looking sound wave that showed enough amplification.

The shape of the waves was erratic, resembling a crowded mountain range with varying peaks and valleys. "Yeah, now this is the one."

The buzzing tone was exciting, like it was fizzing through his blood. Taj turned up the volume and stood up. He duplicated the file and then turned one into a syncopated loop. A heavier bass beat laid down under it. Time was limited before his father knocked on the walls and yelled for him to stop. Taj jumped into his desk chair and cut the rest of the track as quick as he could.

He heard a knock on his door and pressed save with sweaty fingers. "This is the best shit I've ever done."

Taj expected to see his father when he opened his bedroom door, so he actually gasped when he saw his brother's fiancé.

Michelle was mesmerized by something, her head tipped to one side, focused on Taj.

"Mmm, it's coming from your room." Michelle licked her lips.

Taj looked at her glistening cherry-red lipstick and ducked back behind his bedroom door before she could hurl some horrible insult at him.

"Holy shit!" Taj stumbled and fell onto the floor.

His brother's fiancé was dancing, her blonde hair bouncing and generous hips pumping up and down.

Michelle's perfectly manicured fingernails trailed down her neck and then she palmed her breasts. When she saw Taj on the floor, she turned around to give him a better view of her delicious booty.

Then Michelle shimmied into Taj's bedroom.

He stood up, but where could he sit and look casual even if he was getting a total hard-on for his soon-to-be sister-in-law? He selected his desk chair and pretended to work on his music.

Michelle shut his bedroom door. Then she leaned against it and wiggled lower and lower, her breasts bouncing to his beats. Taj tried not to look, but soon his desk chair swung all the way around.

"I don't know what's going on in here, Taj, but I like it," Michelle purred.

She slipped her shirt off and revealed her full breasts barely contained in a pink bra. Taj could see her nipples straining against the lace. Michelle noticed him looking and bounced in rhythm with his music while she unzipped her tight jeans.

Taj gripped the sides of his desk chair, too afraid to reach out to touch Michelle. She was so perfect, so sexy and so off-limits. And she was standing two feet away with a hungry smile, wearing nothing but a pink bra and panties.

"I heard the music from down the hall and it sounded amazing. I'm really loving it." Michelle's hands began to graze her near-naked body.

She teased her nipples to tighter peaks and then knelt down in front of Taj. Her body still gyrated to his music and every now and then Michelle's tight nipples brushed against his knees.

"Where's my brother?" Taj squeaked in a weak voice.

"Mani? Who cares about Mani? This music just feels so good." Michelle put her hands on Taj's thighs and crawled up to straddle his lap. "It's making me so hot, Taj. So hot."

Taj leaned back onto his desk as Michelle rubbed her tits up and down his chest. His elbow hit his laptop and the music stopped.

"Uh, ow." Michelle leaned back and grabbed her head. Then she saw Taj and jumped up. "What? How did I get in here, and where are my clothes?"

"What do you mean?" Taj leapt out of his desk chair as if she'd been keeping him hostage. "You're the one that just danced in here, stripped and wouldn't stop talking about how much you love my new music."

Michelle wriggled back into her clothes as fast as she could. "I don't know what happened. I hate techno!"

Taj panicked and accidentally started the music again.

Michelle dropped her clothes and a look of ecstasy spread over her face. She began twerking, but Taj's interest was caught by something more amazing than his brother's stuck-up fiancé doing a private striptease for him.

On his dresser, Taj had a mini Zen garden. Usually the neglected sand was in dusty lumps, but now it was vibrating. Geometric patterns danced across the humming sand particles. And when he turned the music off, the sand dropped, still in the distinctive patterns.

Michelle groaned and reached for her clothes.

"Sorry, wait, just one more time." Taj turned on the music once more, but he didn't realize how close Michelle was. She grabbed his shoulder and spun him around, her body gyrating up and down on him as she leaned in for a kiss.

"Whoa, Michelle! You really need to get out of here." Taj turned off the music and dodged away from her.

"Ow. Where am I?" Michelle frantically looked around. "This isn't Mani's room. And why are you looking at me like that, Taj?"

She gasped when she looked down and realized she was half-naked. "Oh my god! I don't know what happened but if you tell anyone I'll kill you!" She scooped up her clothes and stormed out of the bedroom before Taj could respond.

"Wow," Taj said. "What was that all about?"

He jumped back into his desk chair and studied everything for a clue. His laptop didn't show anything out of the ordinary. There was nothing odd about the tracks he'd accidentally recorded overnight.

How did he make that sound... and could he make it again?

Juanita, the housekeeper, quietly stepped foot into Taj's room. Before she could say a word, a red light began flashing on Taj's synthesizer keyboard. He cried out when he spotted it. "Yes!"

"Okay, thank you, Mr. Das. I clean while you work." Juanita thought he had just invited her in. She was a beautiful and curvy Latina from Puerto Rico, standing at five feet, two inches with a reserved demeanor.

She started to dust while kicking his dirty clothes into a pile on the floor. Taj shrugged and turned back to his desk.

He double-clicked on a sound from his new track and the sound wave appeared on his screen.

He isolated the frequency that stood out and then played it by itself. The sound was a pleasant midrange hum that evoked a feeling of serenity and produced an almost warm-like feeling over the body.

"This has to be it," Taj said.

He listened again and noticed that Juanita had stopped moving. When he turned around, she was staring over his head with a dreamy smile. Then Juanita focused on Taj and her eyes lit up.

Taj spun back to his laptop and stared at the frequency in confusion. "What is happening?"

The feather duster tickled his ear. Taj yelped and turned to find Juanita's seductive smile only a foot away. She tickled him with the duster again.

"Oh, Mr. Taj, I got you dirty. Here, let me help."

Juanita leaned forward to brush off the dust and let Taj get a good long look down her gaping shirt.

When she stood up and unbuttoned her shirt, Taj pinched himself.

"This can't be a coincidence. This is really happening."

Juanita tossed away her shirt and bra and then let down her thick, shiny hair. Before he could stop the music, Juanita grabbed both of Taj's hands and wrapped them around her backside.

She rubbed his palms onto her ass as her bare breasts bounced in his face. Then she leaned down and kissed him hard.

Taj pried one hand loose and gasped for air between Juanita's insistent kisses. He fumbled over his chair and managed to bash the mute button.

"Oh! Mr. Das, what is going on?"

"It's alright, Juanita. We were just enjoying a passionate kiss. Your bra and shirt are over there on my bed." Taj tried to stay calm.

"Dios mío . Please don't tell your parents!"

"Don't worry, I won't. This is just between you and me."

He tried to go in for another kiss. Juanita was beautiful and unattached as far as Taj knew. What was the harm?

"¡Ay Jesus! ¿Qué pasó?" Juanita yanked on her shirt and ran for the bedroom door.

For a moment, Taj's shoulders slumped again. Juanita had looked so disgusted! Then he remembered the new track waiting on his laptop.

"Hmmm, looks like I might be able to make the ladies dance after all!" Taj grinned and got back to work.

CHAPTER FIVE

PANTY-DROPPING PLAYLIST

"639 hertz?" Taj squinted at his laptop screen. "Can that really be it?" His mind jumped back to the evidence he had just witnessed firsthand. He now knew that Michelle had a small mole just below her right breast. He knew from experience that Juanita liked to use a lot of tongue when kissing.

"Let's face it, the reason wasn't me," Taj muttered.

He remembered how Juanita had pulled away from his attempted kiss when the music was muted. He checked the tone generator again and found the same frequency: 639 hertz.

"Who cares about the science, I'm putting this sound on all of my beats!" Taj cracked his knuckles and hunched over his laptop.

He focused until he was satisfied that every track from his failed DJ debut had been reworked with the mysterious frequency.

Then he stood up and stretched. He looked at the playlist for about ten seconds before he grabbed his phone from the charger and ran out of his bedroom.

He thundered down the stairs and dodged past his scowling brother. "Hey! What'd you say to Michelle? She's pissed about something!"

"Nice to see you, bro. Say goodbye to Michelle for me," Taj called over to his brother. He swung around the corner and through the door to the garage.

The Civic Taj had inherited from his father was so old it was a total junker in all respects except one: Taj had spent every dime he'd saved on a top-of-the-line sound system.

He punched the garage opener and jumped in. Somewhere in the house his father was yelling Taj's name, so he backed out as fast as he could. The antenna of the car scraped the rising garage door, but Taj was safe and on the road before Prasad caught up to him.

It was a sunny, warm day and Taj rolled down all four of the car windows. Birds chirped as he braked at a stop sign and connected his phone to Bluetooth. He grinned at himself in the rearview mirror as the first track started. The birds flew off as Taj cranked the volume and eased through the intersection.

Taj spotted a jogger and headed in her direction. He cruised up to her slowly and admired the view of her behind bouncing along the sidewalk.

Her bright pink running shorts were topped with a purple tank that she suddenly tugged up and over her head. In nothing but her sports bra and tiny shorts, she jogged in place until her head swiveled towards Taj's car.

He cruised by and waved. Then he saw her start to run after his car. Taj watched her bright smile in the rearview mirror. It didn't change even as he sped up to the speed limit. She sprinted behind him until he zoomed through an intersection and left her behind. Taj saw her grab her head and then yank her tank top back on in embarrassment.

"What is going on?" he asked himself.

Next was a mom pushing a toddler in a stroller. She marched along, tired and annoyed, until she got close enough to hear Taj's music. She pried her hands off the stroller handles and waved at Taj. He ogled her bursting breasts and she did a little shimmy to show them off as he drove past. The toddler started to cry as his mother stepped around the stroller and hurried after Taj.

"Oh shit!" Taj exclaimed.

He turned down the volume and she spun around to her child with a horrified look on her face.

Taj pumped the volume back up at the next stop sign and was delighted when a white Volkswagen Beetle pulled up next to him. Three girls rolled down their windows and waved at Taj.

"'Sup, girls. What's happening?" he called.

"Heyyy," they responded in unison with big smiles.

He drove through the stop sign and watched as they cranked out of the turn lane and followed him, the Beetle almost kissing his bumper as he cruised along.

"This is the greatest!" Taj cried.

Then he had to stop at a red light. An elderly neighbor sat on the bus bench and knitted while she waited. When she heard Taj's music, her white eyebrows lifted and she grinned. She dropped her knitting needles and pulled up her shirt to reveal a pair of breasts defeated by the force of gravity.

"Ugh, Mrs. Williams!" Taj hit stop on the playlist as quick as he could.

Luckily the light turned green and Taj sped away from the bus stop. The white Volkswagen Beetle did a U-turn and Taj had the suburban street all to himself. He kept cruising but grabbed his phone instead of turning the music back on.

Skyler D answered after two rings. "Hello?"

"Yo, Skyler, it's Taj."

"Yo. What's up, DJ Buzzkill?" Skyler D chortled at his own joke.

Taj ignored his mockery. "Dude, something unexplainable is happening!"

"What? You're getting your dick wet?"

"Almost. No. But that's not the point!" Taj took a breath and tried to stay focused. "You gotta gimme another chance to DJ at the Pearl. I promise you, this time I'll get all the ladies on the dance floor."

Skyler D snorted. "I don't know, Taj. Last night was so bad. I mean really, really bad. I've never seen a DJ clear the dance floor that fast. Hey! You should totally change your name to DJ Fire Drill!"

Taj waited until his friend was done howling with laughter. "Not cool, dude. Please, you gotta give me another shot."

Skyler hesitated, but gave in. "Alright. One of my openers canceled on me, so I guess you can have his slot. But if you clear the dance floor again this time, then you're done. Got it?"

"Got it!" Taj said.

"Be there tonight, ten o'clock sharp," Skyler told him.

"Okay, I won't let you down." Taj took a breath to tell Skyler about the miracle sound, but his friend stopped him.

"Make sure you get the party jumping, Taj."

"Don't worry, man. All the girls are gonna go—"

Skyler D hung up on Taj before he could say it: "—crazy."

Taj was still cruising when his phone buzzed and wouldn't stop. "Yeah, yeah, I know about the store," he muttered.

He deleted Prasad's nagging text messages and drove to the liquor store. Taj faced his day job and couldn't turn off the engine. How could he work after making such an astonishing discovery?

Taj parked, grabbed his phone and opened the store in a matter of minutes.

He sent his father a pic of the "open" sign and hoped that would be enough to ward off any lectures. Then he connected his playlist into the store's sound system. Seconds after the music started pumping out of the speakers, the bell above the door jangled.

"Hey, ladies," Taj called to the same two girls that had rejected him the other day.

The taller one went to roll her eyes, but her expression changed when she heard the music. The shorter one tossed her soft curls and started to dance toward the counter.

"Heyyy, Taj," the taller one cooed.

"Come dance with us," the shorter one held out her hands as her hips swiveled and dipped.

Taj wiped his sweating palms on his pants and came out

from behind the counter. "Sure thing, sexy ladies, but how about we go somewhere a little more private?"

The taller one nodded enthusiastically as she tore her shirt off over her head. Her friend giggled and pulled Taj toward the back of the store. He escaped long enough to lock the liquor store door before the eager women dragged him into the back storeroom.

The music was muffled in the tight storeroom but that didn't stop the effect. Both ladies stripped off their clothes as their bodies swayed and undulated to his beats. Taj was tossed onto a pile of cardboard recycling. He lay back as the now naked women took turns dancing over and on his lap.

"So, you like my music?" Taj's voice came out in a high squeak.

"Uh huh, it feels so good," the taller one said. She used the corner of a storage shelf like a stripper's pole.

"It makes me want to do more than dance," the shorter one said. She straddled Taj and lowered herself onto his fully clothed body.

Taj white-knuckled a collapsed box of Coors as she continued to gyrate and dance on his lap. How far could his music get him? Her nipples brushed his cheek and Taj hung on tighter, his mouth dropping open.

At the front of the store, someone pounded on the locked door. Taj heard the angry banging but figured whoever it was would just go away. He couldn't answer the door and disappoint two women. Taj was much more considerate than that.

Outside, Prasad paced up and down the sidewalk and then hammered on the liquor store door again. The sign said "open," but he couldn't see Taj inside. Had his son tried to dupe him?

"He'd better be in there somewhere," Prasad muttered.

Taj's father marched back to his car to find his spare key. He continued his tirade about his youngest son as he dug through the glove compartment.

His wife had told him to trust Taj. After all, he'd sent a picture proving that he was at the liquor store as promised. Prasad gritted his teeth. He hated to prove Aashi wrong, but she needed to see Taj was turning into a total failure.

"If I don't stop him from ruining his life, then no one will," Prasad grumbled. He grabbed the spare key and marched back to the liquor store door. "What is that awful sound?"

Taj's father unlocked the door and flung it wide open.

Bottles vibrated on the shelves as Taj's music blared out of the overhead speakers.

It annoyed Prasad as his anger mounted.

"Taj! If you're in here you better get to the counter now and explain yourself. This is your one chance!" Prasad's voice thundered above the rhythmic music.

There were a few seconds of silence between songs, long enough for Prasad to hear strange sounds from the back storeroom. He frowned, hoping he wouldn't find his son doing anything distasteful at work.

"What is that?" Prasad asked. He strode behind the counter and turned off the sound system.

Shrieks erupted from the storeroom. Taj's father jumped at the sudden screeching of multiple female voices.

His son's squeaky, apologetic voice punctuated the women's angry words.

"Hang on, ladies! I'll fix it. The music will be back on in seconds!" Taj burst from the storeroom with his belt undone and shirt collar ripped.

Prasad watched in utter amazement as two naked women shoved past his son and ran out of the liquor store with their clothes flapping over their bare shoulders. Stunned, he leaned down and picked up a pair of turquoise silk panties.

"What are you doing here, Dad? That was almost a threesome. An actual threesome!" Taj slapped his belt back together and braced for an angry lecture.

All his father did was let out a long, slow whistle. "Thank Vishnu. I thought he would never get laid!"

CHAPTER SIX

T aj was back home getting ready for his second-chance gig, an opportunity to redeem himself after his dreadful DJing debut. He kicked his green Crocs out of the way. "I'm not gonna need your luck tonight!"

Instead, he carefully selected a black pair of Crocs and checked himself out in his closet mirror. Designer jeans his mother had bought him, a black T-shirt with some cat hair on it and one of his father's black dress shirts tied around his waist.

Taj pointed at himself in the mirror and winked. "Who needs a gimmick when I look this good?"

He changed his white socks for black ones and then posed in front of the mirror again. Taj gave himself his best flirty smile. "Yo, what's up, girl? I'm Taj. Yeah, that's right. I'm the DJ. Oh, you wanna get a hotel room? Only if you bring a friend, sexy."

Taj chuckled and plucked a few of the cat hairs off his T-shirt. His cat glared at him from under his dresser.

"What? Don't I look good, Sushi?" Taj asked his cat.

Sushi hissed and backed farther under the furniture. Taj frowned and bent down to peek at his cat, but then he noticed the time.

"What do cats know about fashion anyway," Taj muttered as he headed out the door.

He brushed the rest of Sushi's stray hairs off his black T-shirt as he waited for the valet to collect his car outside of the Pearl Nightclub. The Civic's dim clock read 9:50pm, but there was already a line of lovely ladies stretching down the sidewalk.

A valet shuffled over to Taj's car and shook his head. Taj grabbed his laptop bag and got out of the car, already beaming at the crowd he was sure he would wow. The valet shifted the car into drive and a cloud of smoky exhaust exploded out of the tailpipe. Taj watched as the crowd choked and coughed. Almost everyone scowled at him.

Taj just gripped his bag tighter and strutted through the smoke. He made it to the sidewalk before one of the women recognized him.

"Oh, god. Is that guy really going to DJ again? Thank God Skyler D is headlining," she said to her friend.

The crowd closest to the woman checked Taj out and laughed.

He just tipped his chin higher and waved at them as he bypassed the long line. "Just wait, douchebags," Taj said to himself through his tight smile.

Then a muscular arm stopped Taj in his tracks. "Whoa. Hold up, little man. Are you on the list?" the bouncer asked.

"I'm the opening DJ!" Taj pointed to his tiny name on the marquee, squeezed in and misspelled just below Skyler D's towering letters. The bouncer squinted up at it and then back down at Taj, clearly not impressed.

"Belly dancing night is on Mondays," the bouncer said.

Taj juggled his bag and dug out his wallet. He showed the bouncer his name and pointed to the marquee again. "See? I'm Taj. I'm spinning tonight!"

The burly bouncer pulled out a spindly pair of reading glasses, perched them on his nose and squinted at the marquee again.

"They spelled your name wrong, Tan."

"Thanks." Taj snatched back his ID and skirted around the bouncer into the club.

Taj rushed into the Pearl and immediately turned his head away from the glaring bright lights. He bumped into the back hallway before his eyes adjusted to the flickering strobe lights and sweeping lasers. Clouds billowed from the fog machines on stage, drifted over the dance floor and became a heavy haze by the bar. Taj coughed and turned toward the stage.

The crowd was growing, but they were parked in front of the bar and Taj had to push and weave his way through knots of women that didn't even notice him. He finally broke free and dashed across the empty dance floor to climb up on stage.

Taj plugged in his laptop, cued up his new beats and looked at the distant crowd. Every single woman had her back to him, too busy flirting with the men at the bar. Doubt froze his finger just above play.

Skyler D's warning flashed through Taj's mind: "You're gonna have to do a one-eighty to even have a chance to make it as a DJ, bro."

He squeezed his eyes shut and accidentally envisioned his brother's fiancé dancing through his room. The sexy memory faded as he remembered Michelle's disgusted face.

"But I hate techno!" she had screeched.

Taj heard his father's ultimatum echo in his head: "I'm giving you one year to get your act together, or else you're out of here!"

Taj snapped out of the flashbacks and realized he was center stage. He was ready for his big break, but took another long, unsteady breath first.

Below him the fog machine clouds swirled around Skyler D as he scowled at Taj impatiently. Next to him DJ Phatty grinned and gave Taj two thumbs up.

"Alright, Taj. It's now or never!" He forced his finger to press play.

The first beats started with Taj's new sound layered underneath. It only took a few seconds for the frequency to fill the club. The female crowd at the Pearl suddenly perked up.

There was a sudden sloshing of drinks, screaming and shoving as the women flooded onto the dance floor. They rushed the stage and Taj saw his friends' bewildered looks before they were enveloped in the sexy crowd.

Taj blinked in surprise. The excited women on the floor looked up at him with an unfamiliar light in their eyes. Lust. He saw collagen-filled lips being licked and surgically enhanced hips pumping just for him.

Taj rubbed his eyes and looked again. He couldn't believe it, but he liked what he saw. The dance floor was packed with women shoving each other to get closer to the stage.

The bar had emptied with the exception of the owner, who attempted to get a whiskey on the rocks. He yelled when the distracted bartender spilled the whiskey, drenching the counter with the sticky liquid. The owner stumbled back as she sopped up the spilled whiskey and wetted her T-shirt with it.

Even the hottest bartender, the one that had never even looked at Taj, was now fixated on him. She shoved her wet-shirted friend out of the way and climbed onto the bar.

She pointed at the stage with one long red fingernail. Taj gawked as she reeled her pointer finger back in and sucked on it suggestively.

The owner gaped as his soon-to-be manager shimmied up and down above him and shrieked for Taj to come slake her thirst.

All Taj could do was pump his fist in the air. The crowd's excitement undulated in waves, and the amateur DJ rode his success on unsteady legs. He grabbed the equipment table and hung on as the crowd surged below him.

Out on the dance floor, men struggled harder than Taj ever had. One man kept spinning his curvaceous girlfriend back to face him. Her shirt was tugged low and the view was mouth-watering. She would just frown at him and spin back to salivate in Taj's direction. The man couldn't understand and started to sweat as he fought for her attention.

Even the men that surrounded the accommodating Nicky were out of luck. Her normal glance of semi-disgust was gone. Taj skimmed by her lustful look, remembering his previous embarrassment in front of her.

It was soon forgotten as Nicky slipped her slinky tank top down to her waist, tore off her push-up bra, and tossed it at Taj. The lacy thing landed on Taj's head and a roar of enthusiasm ripped through the crowd.

Taj tossed the trophy down to DJ Phatty who cheered

him on over the shrieking cheers. "Go, Taj, go!"

Security guards, most of whom had refused Taj entry to the Pearl at one point or another, shoved their way to the stage.

Women rushed the high ledge and charged at the wings, trying to get closer to Taj. The burly men struggled to hold back the horny wave of females.

Taj kept spinning despite his own confusion. Could the frequency really be doing all this? He scanned the crowd again, half-frightened at the raw sexual frenzy he was causing.

Then he saw her.

Her blue evening gown was formal, almost demure, and that made her stand out.

Taj squinted past the stage lights to admire her long brown hair and dark smiling eyes. She was still in the center of the pulsating crowd, and Taj found himself looking at her again and again to steady himself. Finally, she looked up and met his eyes.

Taj nervously raised his hand and pointed at the beautiful, calming angel. He kissed two fingertips and pointed at her again.

She smiled awkwardly and inched her way forward while staring into his eyes.

The crowd surged around her, and Taj found himself relieved when his set was coming to an end. He grabbed the mic and yelled, "Taj is in this bitch!"

Screams of ecstasy filled the club as Taj's last beats slowly faded away. Skyler D stood just below the stage with his arms crossed tightly over his chest. He stared straight ahead as if he could deny the adoring crowd behind him. DJ Phatty hooted and cheered, but Skyler D scowled.

He was still scowling when Taj edged out from behind the DJ table and called down to the headliner. "I told you I wouldn't let you down! How's that for a 180!?"

Taj's beats disappeared and the regular house music took their place. The transition was off, jarring and off-beat, and the crowd of women was suddenly disoriented. Sweaty women tugged their clothes back into place with confused giggles.

Their smiles turned dreamy as the wild, sexual energy drained back to normal levels.

Bright blushes and shocked stares were now all the women directed at Taj.

He jumped off the stage with his laptop bag and joined his friends.

Skyler D managed a fake smile and a loose hug. "Yeah, Taj. You, um, killed it tonight."

"Oh, man! Did you see the girls? They were getting wild! I've never seen so many tramp stamps at once," Taj exclaimed.

DJ Phatty gave him a congratulatory pat on the back and handed him Nicky's padded bra. "Amazing set, man. Amazing! Not even Skyler gets that kind of love. That was crazier than a BTS concert!"

He and Taj headed to the bar for celebratory drinks, but Skyler D stayed back. He hitched himself onto the stage and stared at the DJ equipment as if he'd find some explanation for his friend's unexpected success.

"Hey, Skyler, were you the one who booked Taj for tonight?" A man hailed Skyler D from the dance floor.

"Hi, Stevie. I didn't know you were here." Stevie was an A-list promoter that Skyler D was familiar with. "Wait until you hear what I've got—"

Stevie cut Skyler D off. "I really just want to know Taj's availability for the next few weeks. I've got some big gigs to fill."

Skyler D went stiff. He glanced over at Taj, then shook his head. "Um, I think he seems to be all booked up already. His main job at his dad's liquor store takes up all his time, you know?"

Stevie snorted. "His day job's history, if you ask me."

"Yeah, but it's like a family thing. His calendar's booked." Skyler D shot Taj a guilty look. "But my schedule is pretty open. Want my demo?"

The promoter shrugged. "Sure. I'll keep you in mind, but you've got to talk Taj into clearing his schedule for me."

Skyler D's scowl returned as he watched Stevie walk away. No one in the club was paying any attention to him and he was the headliner. He marched to the DJ table, cued up his first beat and grabbed the microphone.

"What's up, Pearl! You already know, this is Skyler D! How's everyone doing tonight!?"

Exhausted women and annoyed men moved away from the pumping music. Skyler D watched as his normally packed crowds all found stools at the bar or flopped into booths. Not even one person tapped their feet.

"Woohoo! C'mon, Skyler!" DJ Phatty cheered amongst the few people left scattered on the dance floor.

Skyler D gripped the microphone harder as it let out feedback. "Ladies, where you at? It's your man Skyler D, ready to drop that heat, yo!"

"Yeaaaahhhh!" DJ Phatty let out a big cheer as the janitor swept around him.

CHAPTER SEVEN

MORE THAN A FEELING

Taj looked eagerly around, but many of the women were having trouble meeting his eyes. Their cheeks were still bright pink from the dance floor. Those women that made eye contact with him were puzzled and suspicious.

His success quickly gave way to awkwardness and Taj inched down to the far end of the bar.

There he spotted the lovely woman in the blue dress. The dark satin gleamed under the bar lights and Taj found it hard to look away from the demure sweep of her neckline.

When he did drag his eyes upward, he found her smiling at him with one eyebrow arched. She sipped her drink and smiled at having caught his wandering glance.

Taj wiped his sweaty palms on his pants and dug in his pocket for his phone. He got tangled in his headphones and struggled to arrange them casually around his neck.

"What are you doing?" DJ Phatty asked.

Skyler D's set was loud, louder than usual, but Taj hit play on his beats anyway.

He leaned closer to DJ Phatty who picked up the sound and nodded his head along to Taj's music.

"Here, hold this," Taj said as he handed his laptop bag to Phatty. "I'm gonna try and talk to that girl."

He gave Phatty a thumbs-up and headed toward the pretty woman in blue. In her high heels, she was taller than Taj, but she smiled when he stopped and gazed up at her.

"What's up!" Taj said.

He couldn't hear her over Skyler D's insistent set, but Taj saw her mouth the word "What?"

He leaned closer, hoping his beats would take effect. Taj pulled out his phone and held it up. "Got a number?"

She smiled even as the now restless crowd jostled her. Taj reached out a hand to steady her and they both smiled. He waggled his phone hopefully. As she reached for it, her friend walked up and grabbed her arm.

"Janet, we're leaving. Let's go!" She tugged, trying to get her friend to budge.

Taj stepped forward, still hoping to get the beautiful brown-eyed girl's number. "Wait!"

Janet's friend glared at him and Taj froze. She was definitely in the crowd of confused women that were now shooting him dirty looks. Taj gulped as he recognized her as one of the women that had slipped off her panties and flung them in the air.

"C'mon. Now," Janet's friend insisted.

Janet grabbed Taj's phone, typed her phone number in and then handed it back. She dug into her small purse and pulled out her phone to give to Taj, but before he could reach for it her friend intervened yet again.

"She'll call you." She stuck an arm out to block Taj and accidentally knocked Janet's phone out of her hand. She cried out as a passing group kicked the phone farther away. "Oh, Janet! I'm so sorry!"

Janet's brown eyes widened with despair as her phone dodged around the club floor. She reached for it but her friend pulled her back just before she was trampled.

"I got it!" Taj dove onto the sticky floor.

His hands were trampled twice, he crawled through what he hoped was just beer, and a shocked woman in a miniskirt dropped ice all over his head, but Taj retrieved the phone. He punched his number in with sore fingers and handed it back to Janet.

She texted him immediately: "My hero!"

Taj pressed his phone to his heart and gave her a dazed smile. "No one's ever called me their hero before."

"I can see why," Janet's friend snorted. She eyed his now stained knees and then waved to get her friend's attention. "Can we go now?"

Janet gave a small nod but peeked over her friend's shoulder to smile at Taj one more time.

He quickly typed as they walked away: "Save my number?"

She was almost to the door when she stopped to text back a smiley face.

Taj gave an excited cry and quickly texted: "Btw, what's your email?"

"Janetlovesbass@gmail.com," came the reply. Taj replied with a heart emoji.

"Wow, nice work," DJ Phatty said, reading over Taj's

shoulder. "What are you doing now?"

"I'm sending her one of my new and improved beats. For her listening pleasure," Taj said.

"How's that for a 180?" The two friends high fived like little kids before trying to look cool again.

"That was a great set, Taj. I can call you Taj, right?" Stevie strolled up and stuck out a hand.

Taj resisted the urge to high five again and shook the man's hand. "Wow, man. Nice suit."

Stevie replied, "Thanks, it's Canali. My name is Steven Peterson, but people know me as Stevie."

Stevie handed Taj his equally stylish business card.

"I was really digging your energy up there and the ladies were going crazy for you. I don't know how, but you turned the dance floor into a slip and slide!"

"Yeah, just the way we like it." Taj elbowed DJ Phatty. "The wetter the better!"

Skyler D started yelling into the microphone, trying to get the crowd's attention.

Stevie held out an arm and moved Taj to a quieter corner to talk business.

DJ Phatty followed, though his eyes were on the dance floor. Skyler D's set was nearly over and only a few small groups of women stood around the edges of the dance floor.

"So, I'm organizing events for the Playboy Mansion. It's unfortunate your schedule is so full, but let's keep in touch," Stevie said.

"My schedule?" Taj laughed. "What do you mean?"

"I was talking to your buddy." Stevie jerked his head toward Skyler D. "He mentioned you're really busy at your dad's liquor store."

Taj shot a worried glance at Skyler D. "He did?"

DJ Phatty chuckled. "I'm pretty sure he can find someone to cover his shifts."

Taj's troubled eyes were on Skyler D when DJ Phatty gave him a whack on the back. DJ Phatty's hard hit broke Taj out of his worries. "Here's your bag, I'll let you guys handle biz."

They grinned at each other and DJ Phatty left to check out the few girls left on the dance floor.

"So, you might be free?" Stevie asked.

"Yeah, totally." Taj brightened. "I can clear my schedule. What do you have in mind?"

"I'm coordinating an event at the Mansion next week and I would love to have you DJ. Pays $5,000 for an hour set plus comped bottles. Best of all, you'll be surrounded by the most beautiful women in L.A.! How about it?"

Taj grabbed the promoter's hand and shook it wildly. "Count me in! I'm there for sure!"

"Great." Stevie massaged out his sore hand. "Give me a call tomorrow and I'll have more of the details for you."

"Will do! Thanks a lot, Stevie!"

Taj stood in a daze as the man walked away. The whole night was starting to feel like a dream, and Taj sneaked a hand up his sleeve for a good, hard pinch. It was real. His set had been such a success that he now had a gig at the Playboy Mansion!

His hand immediately raised, looking for anyone to high five.

Two scowling bros at the bar were staring at him, so he smoothly switched to some kind of stretch that looked even stranger.

"After the Playboy Mansion, I won't be left hanging," Taj told himself.

He grinned and scanned the club for DJ Phatty. At least there was one person who would always high five him.

DJ Phatty stood a few feet behind a group of girls. They were swaying their hips to Skyler D's last song but not really dancing. In an attempt to lure them onto the dance floor, DJ Phatty began an awkward version of the robot dance. The girls circled up tighter and pretended they didn't see him.

Taj cringed for DJ Phatty, who continued his robot moves with increasing energy. It was as if someone had shot a current of electricity through a talking stuffed teddy bear.

DJ Phatty finished a particularly awkward arm swinging move that turned into a wave as he caught Taj's gaze. Then he wiped his brow and saluted the group of girls that had continued to ignore him.

"Whew! Good dancing with you, ladies. Same time next week?" The girls inched away from him, frowning as they moved in a tight clump. DJ Phatty was sweating profusely from his energetic display but grinned hopefully even as rivulets poured down his face and splattered his shirt.

The group turned together and marched off the dance floor, leaving DJ Phatty to catch his breath on a long, frustrated sigh.

He shuffled over to join Taj at the edge of the dance floor. "Did you see me working those girls? They couldn't keep up with this dance machine!"

Taj gave DJ Phatty's damp shoulder a light pat. "Yeah, bro. Those were some fresh moves! YouTube?"

DJ Phatty grinned and finally mopped his flooded forehead with his sleeve. "You know it! Though it's a lot harder than it looks."

They both headed back to the bar and caught Skyler D leaning there with an empty shot glass and deep scowl on his face. His set had finished with no one noticing.

Oblivious, Taj gave him a playful punch. "Great set tonight!"

Skyler D gave Taj a half-hearted grin and tried to swivel away only to run right into the still-sweating DJ Phatty.

"Yeah, man. Great set. I really got some girls going with my new moves."

Skyler D couldn't help himself. He met Taj's glance and they both repressed smiles. There was still a tense set to Skyler D's shoulders, but it soon broke as DJ Phatty proceeded to pat his forehead dry with bar napkins that left little stuck pieces all over his face.

"So you staying out to close the deal with those girls?" Skyler D asked him.

"Nah. I'm pretty tired now. Plus, I've gotta stop by the store on my way home and buy my mom a lottery ticket. Catch you guys later." DJ Phatty wandered off toward the club doors, muttering to himself. "Hmm. I wonder if the hot dog lady is here already. I smell bacon!"

Taj watched him go until Skyler D stuck a sharp elbow in his ribs. "Hey, so I saw you talking to Stevie during my set. How'd that go?"

"Oh, you know," Taj said, trying to contain his smile. He leaned back casually on the bar, but his cool attitude lasted all of five seconds. "I got a gig at the Playboy Mansion!"

Taj's joyful outburst made Skyler D take a step backward. "Really?" he asked.

"Yup! And he offered me $5,000 to DJ there next week. At the freaking Playboy Mansion, dude!"

Skyler D's mouth went slack for a few seconds, and he

studied the edge of the bar in disbelief. That gig should have been his. Finally, he mustered enough energy to return a fraction of Taj's bright excitement. "No fucking way!"

Taj, in his joy, did not notice. "Dude! I told you the ladies would be dancing to my beats! Oh yeah, who's the man? Taj is in this muthafucka!"

Taj raised both hands and marched up and down the bar in a victory lap.

His friend shoved his stool hard into the bar and then headed for the doors. Taj called goodbye to him, but Skyler D only waved over his shoulder and kept going.

"I'm the man," Taj said to himself.

He looked around the club just in case someone else wanted to celebrate with him, but the place had emptied out fast. Undeterred, Taj headed for the door and practically skipped toward the valet attendant.

CHAPTER EIGHT

THE TASTE OF VICTORY

Taj's excitement over his success continued despite the rough grinding sound his car made when it started. He had thought about cruising around and listening to his own beats, but the heaving coughs of the engine directed him straight home.

"At least we gotta stop for a Victory Burrito," Taj told his POS car. "All those women salivating over me has got me hungry!"

Even saying it out loud did not make his set at the Pearl feel any more real. He wished the club could have stayed open later than usual, so he could hang on to the reality of the night for a little longer. As he pulled his spluttering car into the Bandido's parking lot, Taj couldn't help but wonder if the night had been one long dream.

High off the success of the night and distracted, he almost drove right into the fast-food intercom. He rolled down his window and waited but there was no crackling, muted voice to greet him. He checked the clock and saw it read 1:55am.

"Hello?" Taj called.

Taj drummed his fingers on the steering wheel as he anxiously waited for a response...

A minute later the intercom was still silent, and Taj drove around the corner to the window that was already closed. He had to crane his head out his open car window to peek inside. The cashier was scrubbing down the counter and trying to ignore Taj until he tapped on the window.

Annoyed, the cashier opened up.

"Estamos cerrados. We closed!" Then he tried to slam the window shut.

Taj stuck his hand inside to stop him. "Come on, bro! I have four more minutes."

"The cook put the food away," the cashier said.

He pulled the window farther closed but didn't have the heart to crush Taj's fingers.

"I always come here! Please. I need my Victory Burrito to cap off my night!" Taj threw his car in park and climbed farther out to peek past the cashier. "Is Carlos back there? He makes the best ones."

The cashier scratched under his chin and shrugged. He turned around and flagged down the cook. "Oye, Carlos. Que es un pinche Victory Burrito?"

Carlos reluctantly turned down his afterhours music and made the cashier repeat the question. Then he gave a sly smile and nodded. "Must be Taj. Secret menu shit. Charge him $4.99."

The cashier raised both eyebrows as he turned and grinned back at Taj. "Okay, is $6.99."

"Yes!" Taj's stomach growled ferociously as he waved to the cook. "Thanks, Carlos! You're the man!"

"You got it, Taj." Carlos snorted and gave Taj a sarcastic thumbs-up. He turned to the grill and muttered under his breath. "This fucker always ordering at the last minute."

Taj jumped back into his front seat and dug out the money. "A little pricier than I remember."

He handed it to the distracted cashier who almost dropped the handful of loose change. "Yeah, we charge a late fee now."

Carlos proceeded to make Taj's burrito by taking a big spoon and scraping the bottom of the nearly empty trays.

"You must be new here." Taj squinted up to read the cashier's nametag. "Robert. My name is Taj. I come here all the time."

"Yeah, I just started two days ago," Robert said. He pretended not to notice as the cook slopped all the ugly leftovers onto a stale tortilla and rolled it into a lumpy burrito.

"Cool!" Taj drummed on his steering wheel again.

"They already promoted me to executive assistant point-of-sale operator," Robert told him.

"Congrats, Robert," Taj said. "Hey, maybe one day you'll own this place!"

The cashier got a faraway look in his eyes. "One day…"

"Victory Burrito's ready!" Carlos called. He handed Robert the misshapen burrito wrapped in leaking tinfoil.

The cashier dropped it in a bag and handed it out the window to Taj. "Enjoy your burrito, Haj."

Clueless, Taj leaned far out of his window to wave again. "Thanks, Robert! Thanks, Carlos!"

Carlos shuffled over to the fast-food window and gave Taj a smile. "Welcome, Taj. Have a good night."

"I love Bandidos!" Taj cried as he shifted into drive.

Carlos and Robert watched as Taj's car left the parking lot and headed down the street.

"What the fuck is a Victory Burrito?" Robert asked.

Carlos snorted again. "Whatever the fuck I feel like putting in there. It's always different and I don't know why he keeps ordering it. They've got to be giving him the shits."

"Maybe he knows something we don't," Robert said. He wiped down the same section of the counter for the fifth time. "Ey, make me one, yeah?"

"One of Taj's Victory Burritos?" Carlos stared at the new cashier. "You saw what I did, right?"

Robert nodded, his hopeful smile still bright. "Maybe it's really good."

Carlos shook his head in frustration. "Just finish cleaning up, Mr. Executive Assistant."

Down the street, Taj was already eating his burrito. He frowned as he chewed, then pulled up at a stop sign and spit something hard out the window. There was only a momentary pause at the intersection before he took another bite and drove home. By the time he pulled into the driveway, the burrito was gone and Taj was still smiling.

The house looked dark and foreboding until Taj slipped in the side door with his laptop bag in hand. His mother had left a hallway light on for him. He turned the lights off, took a few steps and stumbled over a stack of his father's inventory catalogues. The slippery covers made Taj lose his balance and, before dropping hard to his knees, he clutched his bag to protect it from the floor. He got up in pain but was relieved his laptop was safe. "Phew... That was close."

Upstairs, he quickly brushed his teeth and fell asleep almost as soon as he flopped into bed. Soon after, he began having a dream. The dream began in the middle, otherwise Taj never would've imagined a woman in bed with him. He had no idea how they'd gotten there but she was cuddled up next to him as if it was something they did every night.

Her hair tickled his face and, in the dream, Taj tried to smooth it back. Was it the pretty woman in the dark blue dress? She stirred in her imaginary sleep and Taj held still, not wanting the dream to fade.

Then the fantasy woman slipped out of Taj's bed and stood up. His pulse roared as the image of sexy lace lingerie raised his sleeping heart rate.

She smoothed it over her tight body, but Taj still couldn't see her face. In the dream, he sat up and tried to catch her hand. The woman giggled and stepped just out of reach. She refused to turn around and walked slowly toward the door.

Taj waited a moment, just to appreciate the dream's juicy backside, but then he felt his heart squeeze. She was leaving!

"Where are you going? Don't leave me!" Taj cried.

Taj had to wrestle with his covers even in the dream, and by the time he flopped out of his tangled bed, the fantasy woman had slipped through the door. Relieved to see that it was still open, Taj stumbled across the floor.

He stopped and clung to the doorframe as the dream changed. Jungle trees closed in on the other side and Taj saw heavy vines hanging down over his head.

The jungle pulsed with a humid breeze that seemed to beckon Taj through the door. He stepped through and a rough path appeared.

Struggling through the canopy of vines and tightly growing trees, Taj pushed through the jungle. The twisting trail led to a small clearing where Taj saw a single tent. Smoke billowed out the top and filled the grove with a drifting haze.

Taj was hesitant, but the mystery of the tent drew him closer. When he stood in front of the tent's curtain entrance, Taj tried to shut his eyes, but it was impossible. The curtain shifted aside, moved by an unseen force.

"Hello?" Taj asked.

A lone figure in a white robe sat with his back to the entrance. Gray hair reached the man's shoulders and gave Taj an uncomfortable sense of eternity.

As Taj's uncontrollable footsteps led him around the edge of the tent, he saw the man had a long, flowing white beard. It hung down over the man's legs, wrapped in a yoga prayer position, and reached all the way to a woven rug.

The man remained still, his eyes closed.

Taj swallowed hard and felt just how real the dream had become. The heavy scent of incense made him dizzy, and he could hear the same buzzing sound he had recorded under his beats.

Ebbing and flowing over the steady frequency was the sound of Indian sitars.

"Hello?" Taj asked again.

He leaned forward, wondering if the man was sleeping or maybe meditating. Deep age lines obscured his face and Taj crept closer to the man to see if he was even breathing.

Man, I've never seen so many wrinkles, thought Taj.

He waved his hand in front of the ancient man's face. Nothing. He knelt down and inched closer. Now Taj held his breath, intent on discovering if this dream image was a real man or not.

Wide, clear eyes flew open and looked straight into Taj's soul.

He woke from the dream, sweating and gasping for air. He tossed off his tangled covers with a deep groan, then farted.

"Ugh, what was in that burrito?"

When Taj struggled to sit up, he was facing an old poster his mother had given him. It depicted the seven chakras of the human body as glowing orbs of light down the center of a seated man. Taj rubbed his eyes and noticed the poster illustration was sitting in the same yoga prayer position as the figure in his dream.

His chest hurt and Taj rubbed it, his eyes naturally going to the heart chakra on the poster.

He peered closer at Anahata, the heart chakra, and noticed a small notation underneath the glowing orb. Each chakra was associated with a specific vibration in a delicate font Taj had never noticed before.

Taj scratched his head. "639 hertz?"

CHAPTER NINE

RISING STOCK

A week later, Taj was standing in front of his closet at a complete loss for what to wear to the Playboy Mansion. He grabbed another random selection of shirts, including one that had gold stripes and another that was solid turquoise and tossed them on his bed.

"You seem like a lucky color," Taj told the turquoise shirt. He held it up and looked in the mirror. The vibrant color turned his skin a sickly shade of green and he tossed it onto the towering reject pile.

It was a relief when his phone buzzed and Taj was able to step away from the stress of getting dressed for his big event.

Stress turned into excitement as Taj saw a text message from Janet. The girl in the blue dress hadn't deleted his number!

"Hey, remember me? :)" her text said.

Taj gripped his phone and responded immediately. "Of course! We met last week at the Pearl!"

He almost fumbled his phone, overjoyed when she texted right back: "Thought u wouldn't remember... You've been on my mind since we met :) LOL."

Taj watched, mouth gaping, as Janet sent a ten-second video of her puckering her lips in a kiss. The message disappeared seconds later, but Taj's surprised grin stayed in place for a lot longer.

He replied, ":) Stoked to hear from you! Loved that vid. I miss your face. What's your IG, beautiful?"

"It's @SweetJanet_86."

"Okay, cool. I'm going to follow you, but let's hang soon!" Taj texted.

Janet responded moments later. "Yeah, I would really like that ;) I'm leaving for a family trip next week so I'll let you know when I get back. Btw, I've been playing that beat u emailed me over and over. Loving the bass!"

Taj's palms were sweating with excitement, but he managed to text back: "Thanks! Glad you like it! Hope you have a great trip!"

He waited, holding his breath, but their text message conversation was over. Taj raced to log on to Instagram and follow Janet. Leaning close to the screen to see every detail, Taj pressed like on all of her pictures. He especially admired her pictures of food and art.

"She's got great taste. Maybe I should ask her to help me pick out a shirt," Taj suggested out loud to himself.

He was about to text her again when there was a knock on his door.

"Taj, do you have a minute?" Prasad asked.

Taj bit his lip as the clothes pile slipped off his chair and spilled at his father's feet. "I'm kinda busy," he said.

Prasad arched an eyebrow at his son, stepping over the mound of clothes. "I just wanted to let you know that I talked to my friend Nadir."

"Cool, but I really should be getting ready. I have a big gig tonight, remember?"

Prasad dismissed Taj's plans with a wave of his hand, then said, "Nadir has agreed to let you interview for a job at his factory."

"What?" Taj dropped the shirt with the gold stripes and shot his father a disgusted look.

"They have an entry-level position open in the mechanics department and the interview is all set up," Prasad said.

"Why?" Taj howled.

His father crossed his arms over his chest. "You were complaining about working at the liquor store. This is an excellent job that will lead to a real career. I told Nadir you would be very interested."

"No, Dad, I'm not interested. That's not what I want to do with my life!"

Prasad tipped his nose in the air while his stern eyes took in Taj's messy bedroom. "I don't want you to ruin your life any further.

"It's impossible to survive just making music, and you must grow up. You need to think about your future, Taj."

Taj gripped his hair then gestured to his computer. "This is my future! I'm DJing at the Playboy Mansion and getting paid for it! It's the opportunity of a lifetime and my dreams are finally coming true."

Taj's father shook his head sadly. "Listen to me, son. I had dreams too. I wanted to be a Bollywood actor, but when your mom got pregnant I had to get a real job. I had to provide for our family, and that meant giving up my dream for something real, something practical."

Stifling a growl of frustration, Taj grabbed the gold-striped shirt and yanked it over his head. He took a long deep breath. "Dad, I love you, and of course I'm grateful for everything you have done for us. But why can't you understand? I'm not going to be an engineer. I'm not Mani! I'm going to DJ whether you like it or not."

Prasad threw his hands in the air, then poked a finger into his son's chest. "Okay, Taj, you have to learn the hard way. If you will not respect my wishes and listen to me, you'll need to start paying rent. Next month you pay rent or you find somewhere else to live. This is for your own good."

Taj slapped his father's hand away angrily. "Well, since I'm just your tenant now, I'm not working at the store anymore!"

Prasad's temper flared. "What did you say?"

"You heard me, I quit," Taj exclaimed.

"How dare you turn your back on the family business!" Prasad yelled.

Taj rolled his eyes. "Whatever. I'm late for my performance. I'm sorry but I really don't have time for this!"

He grabbed his laptop and stormed out of the room, leaving his father standing in the pile of rejected clothes.

Taj got into his car and began driving.

The confrontation left a tight knot in Taj's chest, but it was soon replaced by excitement. It was hard to take his father's warning about dreams seriously when he was headed to a Playboy Mansion party.

He arrived at the legendary mansion and was greeted

by a security guard with a look of suspicion. "Can I help you, sir?"

"Yeah, I'm the DJ. Stevie hired me. I'm Taj Das."

The guard took a few steps back and began talking on his radio. A few moments later he walked back up to Taj's car.

"Ok Mr. Das, you can pull up right over there and the valet will take your car."

"Awesome, thanks!" exclaimed Taj.

He drove around the driveway and got out of the car with his laptop.

"You might need to put a little muscle into it when you shift into drive," Taj said to the valet attendant as he handed him the keys.

"Sure thing, sir," replied the attendant with a puzzled look.

Once inside, there were Playboy Bunnies in swimsuits, impossibly short dresses and a few in nothing but glossy body paint. His father's stern frown was soon forgotten.

Taj felt out of place until an unimpressed security guard led him to the stage. They carved through the dizzying soiree of celebrities, athletes and models.

Taj's eyes lit up with the sight of all the famous guests. They arrived at the stage and the guard pointed to the staircase.

"Thanks, bro," said Taj, with a bright smile.

The guard rolled his eyes and walked away. Taj nervously walked up the stairs. Once on stage, he realized who was DJing the party.

"Whoa, Nick Skies!" exclaimed Taj.

He was contemptuously greeted by Nick who was closing out his set. Nick was a well-known DJ, especially in the celebrity world. The fact that Stevie had Taj, an unknown

DJ, going on after Nick was a major hit to his ego and really irritated the veteran DJ.

Taj leaned in close to Nick and shouted over the blaring music, "It's an honor to meet you! I'm Taj, Stevie booked me."

He yelled back, "Are you ready to go?"

Taj raised up the laptop in his hand. "Yeah!" he exclaimed. He hurriedly opened his computer and turned it on.

Nick handed Taj a cable as he asked, "What's your name again?"

"Taj!" he replied.

Nick nodded and said, "Alright, you're on." He grabbed the microphone as he cut his music off with everyone cheering in the crowd.

"Thank you everyone! I love you beautiful people," he gleefully exclaimed. He soaked in the crowd's adoration for a few more seconds.

"Alright everyone, now give it up for DJ Hadji!"

The once cheering crowd now looked at each other in puzzlement.

The cheer had been reduced to sparse clapping and confused murmurs. Nick put the microphone down and smirked at Taj as he walked away.

"Good luck, Hadji," he said with a spiteful smile.

Taj didn't have time to dwell on the sabotaged name and introduction. He gave a nervous smile and wave to the crowd, held his breath, and hit play.

Within seconds the miracle happened again. Taj's beats pumped out of speakers throughout the garden and women came running from all corners. The men with dates were now lone soldiers. The enchanted women were determined to get closer to Taj. A muscular one bullied her way through the crowd and even pushed an unsuspecting victim into a fondue fountain. Chocolate splashed everywhere, but no one batted a fake eyelash.

By the second song, all the women from the party were climbing over each other to get to Taj. The ones who made it on stage covered Taj in bright puckers of lipstick and at least four of the sexiest women Taj had ever seen were massaging his shoulders together. He relished in the moment and closed his eyes for a brief second.

A stiff grip suddenly snapped him out of the euphoria as he looked over his shoulders. The soft hands of the women were replaced by two gigantic ones.

He quickly turned around and was met with a sloppy kiss from the towering muscular woman. Before Taj could say anything, she pulled out a champagne bottle and sprayed it over the crowd. With the empty bottle in hand, she blew Taj one last kiss.

As a show of crazed adoration, she broke the bottle over her head, knocking herself out.

Taj was stunned. "What the fuck was that!? That shit was incredible! Wooooooo!" He yelled and screamed as the roar of the crowd grew louder.

Taj regained his focus and continued rocking the party. A sense of confidence grew with every track he dropped. His nerdy slouch transformed into a proud stance as he gazed over the celebration.

"I love this shit," Taj said excitedly. "I was born for this!"

The sight was incredible, and Taj could barely believe it was real. His time had finally come.

He still wasn't sure it was more than a wet dream when his performance was over. He escaped the slightly confused women, slipped backstage and headed to the green room inside the mansion. Inside, he walked past the massive front doors where a huge portrait of Hugh Hefner in his signature robe caught Taj's attention.

"Well, hello, sir." Taj paused in admiration and spoke directly to the painting as if he was there in person. "You were always surrounded by beautiful women. How did you do it? I wish I was more like you."

Hugh's face suddenly distorted and morphed into the mysterious yogi, who stared at Taj with a stern expression. He gasped and stepped back, but the penetrating face remained.

"Taj, you are headed down the wrong path," the yogi warned. Just then, Hugh's son Cooper came into the room and the yogi's face vanished.

Cooper gazed up at his father's portrait and said, "The man that built an empire, a true visionary. He would have gotten a kick out of seeing you perform. You sure have a way with the ladies!"

Taj smiled gleefully, sure to remember Cooper's compliment forever.

"So, what do you think about doing an interview for the magazine?" Cooper asked.

"Who, me?" Taj questioned himself. "Wow, I'd be honored!"

They shook on it and Cooper returned to the party. Taj continued on to the green room. Once inside, he found himself in an opulent setting with a personal bartender catering to his every need. Taj didn't let himself smile until he had his favorite drink in hand. He put his laptop on the plush sofa, sat down and took a slurp of his piña colada. The drink dribbled down his chin and onto his gold-striped shirt.

A flamboyant man in a tailored Armani jacket flew into the room. "Hadji! Wow! That was terrific!"

Taj barely had time to put down his drink before the man pounced. He shook Taj's hand, let the grip linger just a little too long and then introduced himself. "My name's Lance, and I am very happy to meet you."

"Nice to meet you too, Lance, but my name is Taj, not Hadji. That Nick Skies is a real asshole."

Taj scooted a few inches down the sofa as Lance continued to stand over him and look him up and down.

"Well, Taj, you were incredible tonight!" said Lance excitedly.

The bartender recognized the man and brought over an umbrella drink immediately. Lance tucked a hefty tip into the bartender's shirt and then patted his behind as he returned to the bar.

"You really know how to rock a party!" Lance sipped his frothy drink and licked his lips. "I'm a booking agent for some of the hottest clubs in Vegas. You ever perform out there?"

Taj's eyes widened and he quickly stood up. "Sin City!? No, but I stayed at Circus Circus with my parents once."

"You're so cute!" Lance tittered. "Well… are you ready to take over Vegas? I've got a slot opening for Tiesto next month at XS Nightclub."

Taj could see a billboard of himself all lit up over the Las Vegas Strip. He nodded enthusiastically and gave Lance's manicured hand a sweaty handshake. "I was born ready!"

CHAPTER TEN

PAT DOWN

A week had passed since Taj's Playboy Mansion gig. Skyler D and Phatty were at a trendy West Hollywood restaurant waiting for Taj to arrive. Skyler D scanned Sunset Boulevard and then scowled down at his food.

They sat outside at the restaurant where everyone, from the people at the tables to the bus boys to the pedestrians walking by, was hoping to be noticed.

"Where's Taj? He was supposed to be here an hour ago," Skyler D said.

DJ Phatty gazed longingly at his plate. "This food is too good to let it get cold."

"And too expensive," Skyler D snapped.

"I can't wait any longer!" DJ Phatty cried.

Skyler D stabbed a forkful of cold pasta. "An hour late!

What the fuck!?"

"I know, it's not like him." DJ Phatty talked with his mouth full. "He's not returning my calls or texts, either."

"Yeah, ever since he landed that gig at the Playboy Mansion, Taj has been acting like he's the shit," Skyler D said.

DJ Phatty belched and then shrugged, wanting to give his friend the benefit of the doubt. "I don't know, man. Maybe he's just stuck in traffic."

Skyler D opened his mouth to respond but froze. His fork clattered to his plate as a wave of bass-heavy music barreled toward them. A black Lamborghini convertible ripped through traffic, and the music got louder as it got closer to the restaurant. The traffic light turned red at the corner next to the restaurant and the car screeched to a stop.

"What the fuck?" Skyler D pointed to the convertible with a shaky finger.

A young man with oversized sunglasses leaned his wild black hair back on the leather headrest. His grin was open-mouthed and idiotic, and the friends immediately recognized Taj.

"Dude, whose car is that?" DJ Phatty took another bite of food, but his eyes were riveted to the car.

"What a douche. It's probably a rental," Skyler D said loudly.

Taj let out a high-pitched giggle and a blonde head popped up. The woman in the passenger seat looked around for a second and then spit out of the Lamborghini. The white projectile splattered onto the back window of a parked car.

Skyler D threw his napkin on the table and picked up a butter knife. "Did she just spit nut on my car!?"

Phatty started laughing and nearly choked on his food.

Before he could fling silverware at the Lamborghini, the light turned green and Taj peeled off. Skyler D slumped back into his seat and faced an equally shocked but still-chewing DJ Phatty.

The waitress strolled up and gave them a look that said she didn't expect much of a tip. "Can I get you anything else?"

"Just the check," Skyler D said.

DJ Phatty swallowed a big bite. "Actually, miss? Can I see a dessert menu, please?"

Taj sped farther down the street and thought about how he could definitely get used to driving a Lamborghini. The young, blonde Playboy Bunny in the passenger seat wiped her lips with the back of her hand. Taj turned the music up and she immediately started stroking his thigh again.

"Your music makes me so wet," she said. She tugged Taj's hand off the steering wheel and aimed it toward the hem of her very short dress.

The horny Bunny lifted her leg up, eagerly giving Taj full access, but her knee bumped the dashboard.

The music stopped, and so did her guiding hand.

"Oh, shit!" Taj yanked his hand free and frantically pushed buttons to turn the music back on.

It was too late. The Playboy Bunny snapped out of her trance. At first she was disoriented and shook her bright blonde head. Then she whipped back her hair and gave Taj a horrified, confused look.

"Wait, why are you driving my car!? Where are you taking me?"

Taj gripped the steering wheel and punched buttons while he tried to explain. "Okay, Natasha, calm down for a second! Remember, you told me to hop in the driver's seat." Taj's voice raised along with his panic. "And we were headed to your place." Did she really not remember?

"My place? Uh, I think I'll get out right here."

She scrabbled at the passenger side door of the moving car and leaped out.

Taj pulled over to the sidewalk and got out to go after her.

Natasha picked herself up from the street, stumbled her way onto the sidewalk and took off in the opposite direction.

"Hey, wait up! This is your car!" Taj yelled.

Natasha never looked back. Taj shut the passenger door and quickly hopped back into the vehicle. He made a U-turn at top speed and was surprised when he instantly heard the wail of a police siren. Bright flashing lights filled the Lamborghini's rear-view mirror.

A commanding female voice sounded over the squad car's loudspeaker. "Pull over. I repeat, pull over!"

"No, no, no. Not now!" Taj's hands slipped on the steering wheel as he began to sweat profusely.

Somehow he managed to pull the Lamborghini safely to the side of the road. The police officer pulled up behind him and Taj could hear her K-9 partner barking furiously. A muscular female cop got out and approached Taj slowly.

"Oh, god, oh, god. Where is the volume?" Taj reached for the dashboard again.

Next to the car, the officer pulled out her gun. "Freeze! Do not move!"

Taj froze in a cartoonish pose of fear. He only dared to turn his head enough to give the officer a weak smile.

"Um, hi, Officer, ah…" Taj glanced at the officer's nametag. "Morrison. What seems to be the problem?"

"Put your hands where I can see them!" Officer Morrison moved to the door, her gun aimed at Taj's sweaty head.

Taj moved his shaky hands, flat palms out, to either side of his chin, looking more like a scolded child than a street racer.

Officer Morrison was not impressed. "Slowly, and I mean very slowly, step out of your vehicle."

"Okay, don't shoot!" Taj fumbled with the door handle and slipped out of the black Lamborghini.

"Put your hands behind your head and interlock your fingers!" Officer Morrison growled.

Taj did as he was told and cried out when Officer Morrison slapped a pair of handcuffs on him. Then he stood, hands bound behind his back, while she pulled out a flashlight and scanned the interior of the car.

"You on drugs?" she asked, flashing the light in Taj's eyes.

"No, ma'am."

The cop snorted and leaned down into the car to search for evidence he was lying. As she rummaged around, her arm bumped the dashboard and the stereo system kicked back on. Taj's music pulsed out of the high-end speakers and Officer Morrison stopped her search. She slid back out of the low car and smiled at Taj.

"Cool music," she said.

"Um, why thank you, Officer. I made it myself." Taj tried to look charming despite the handcuffs.

She looked him up and down as she licked her chapped lips. "The name's Patty," she said seductively in a husky voice.

"Uh, I'm Taj." His voice squeaked as Officer Morrison pulled out her baton and gave him a mischievous smile.

"Well, you've been a bad boy, haven't you, Taj?" she said as she repeatedly smacked the baton on her masculine hand. "I'm giving you two options, you can go to jail, or..."

A few moments later a couple strolled down the sidewalk with their spoiled Pekingese.

"That Lamborghini is so last year," the man said.

The couple crossed the street a little quicker as the sports car began to rock back and forth. Inside, Taj reclined back painfully on his still-handcuffed arms while Officer Morrison straddled him.

She gripped the steering wheel and rode him aggressively while his music continued to blare.

"Oh, god, no. Ow!" Taj whimpered.

Officer Morrison bounced harder as she began to climax. "Yes, yes, yes! You have the right to remain silent! Anything you say, oh fuuuuccck, I'm cumming !"

CHAPTER ELEVEN

UNSUPPORTED EVIDENCE

The wild night in the Lamborghini had come to an end and Taj was now home. He tiredly made his way up to his room. There was a lot to ponder, but one overriding question begged for an answer: What was the reason he discovered this frequency?

He wondered if it was all just a coincidence, or if there was something bigger at work. Taj buried his head under his pillow and willed his dream to return to the strange yogi in the tent. Maybe he knew something about how Taj's music worked? Maybe he could tell Taj how to control its power?

"Please, yogi, reappear," Taj muttered into his mattress.

He focused and wished as he fell asleep. He tossed and turned all night but only heard the old man's distant laughter.

And then Taj heard the doorbell ringing. He fully awoke as a wave of fear washed over him. What if it was the lady cop?

Night had turned day as Taj flung his pillow off and scrambled out of bed to the window. His blurry eyes told him nothing except neither car in the driveway was a squad car. He rubbed his eyes and looked down to discover he was still in the same clothes as last night. With a shrug, Taj stumbled downstairs to the front door.

"Now what?"

He looked through the peephole and saw Skyler D's angry face. Behind him, DJ Phatty wrung his hands. As Taj tried to decide whether or not to answer the door, Skyler D pressed his eyeball against the peephole.

"We know you're in there, Taj!"

"Shit," Taj muttered under his breath. He tried to smooth his tired face into a smile.

He pulled open the front door and said, "Yo, um, what's up, guys?"

"What the hell happened to you last night?" Skyler D said angrily as he barged into Taj's house. "You were supposed to meet us at the restaurant!"

Taj shut the door behind a sheepish DJ Phatty. "Uh, well, I was working on a new mix and I got tired. Guess I fell asleep early. Sorry for flaking."

Skyler D confronted Taj with his arms crossed over his chest. "Bullshit, bro. You were getting your dick sucked in that Lambo that's parked in your driveway."

Taj frowned and shook his head in denial. He sidestepped Skyler D toward the stairs but DJ Phatty stopped him. "We saw you last night on Sunset Boulevard. Who was that hottie? Is she into robots?"

Taj inhaled slowly and then let out a big breath. "Okay, guys. I have something important to tell you, but we have to go upstairs."

His friends followed him up the stairs and into his bedroom where Taj swept the mound of rejected clothes off his chair.

Skyler D sneaked past DJ Phatty and stole the chair, leaving Phatty to lean against the wall.

Taj sat down at his desk and spun to face them. "So, you know those beats I was playing at the Pearl the other night?"

"Yeah, man." DJ Phatty nodded encouragingly, his double chin bobbing.

"What about 'em?" Skyler D narrowed his eyes.

Taj rubbed his sweaty palms on his thighs. "Well, a couple of weeks ago, I was working on one of those beats really late at night. I guess I kinda dozed off on the keys. When I woke up there was this weird buzzing sound coming from my speakers."

Skyler D faked a yawn, clearly not believing Taj.

"No, really!" Taj cried. "I didn't know what it was, but whenever I play it, it starts raining pussy!"

Even DJ Phatty looked skeptical. "Some kind of buzzing sound?"

"Seriously!" Taj said. "The first time I played it, my brother's fiancé came in here and started taking her clothes off as soon as she heard it."

Skyler D let out a whistle. "Dirty fantasy, but Michelle does have a nice rack."

"It wasn't a fantasy! When I stopped the music, she was acting all disoriented and couldn't remember how she got in my room. Then I pressed play again and Michelle pushed me up against my desk and tried to fucking kiss me!" Taj's chest heaved as he looked from friend to friend, hoping they would believe him.

DJ Phatty scratched his belly. "Wait, let me get this straight. Your brother's super-hot fiancé Michelle tried to kiss you?"

Taj couldn't even be offended by his friend's incredulous tone. "I know. Crazy, right? I finally got her out of my room before anyone saw. Then, a few minutes later, the same shit went down with Juanita, our housekeeper!"

"Damn, bro. Since when did you become such a bull-shitter?" Skyler D asked.

"I know. Just keep it real, man." DJ Phatty looked sad. "You don't have to lie to us, we're your friends."

"Dude, I'm being fucking serious!" Taj flopped down on his bed. "I discovered some sort of..." He hesitated. "I don't know, a love frequency? When my beats are playing, no ladies can resist me!"

Skyler D laughed. "There's no way. A *love* frequency? You mean, like the 'Brown note'?"

Taj grabbed his pillow and shrieked into it before sitting up and trying to explain it all again. "No! Girls don't shit themselves, dude. Why don't you guys believe me?" Taj was growing more frustrated. "After Juanita left my room, I got in my car and drove around the block. I had my music bumping and girls were practically throwing themselves at me. My neighbor's grandma even showed me her titties!"

DJ Phatty groaned. "Ugh, Mrs. Williams? How did they look?"

"Guys, you saw what happened at the Pearl during my last show. I had girls going crazy! They were all over my nuts!" Taj exclaimed.

"That night was a fluke," Skyler D snapped. "And you just got lucky that Stevie happened to be there."

"Well, how do you explain the Lambo and the Playboy Bunny?" Taj asked.

His friends paused, unable to deny what they had seen.

"And I got invited to open for Tiesto in Vegas next month!"

Skyler D slumped back in his chair. "Tiesto? Really?"

DJ Phatty busted out a few robot moves. "Vegas? No way, that's huge, Taj! Congrats, bro!"

"Thanks, Phatty," Taj said. He stood up. "And to make up for flaking last night, I want you guys to go with me. All expenses paid! You're going to see this is for real."

"I love Vegas. Can we hit the big buffets?" DJ Phatty asked.

Taj laughed. "Of course. We'll go to the best ones! I'll even get you a front-of-the-line pass. How about it, Skyler? You in?"

Skyler D frowned and stared down at his hands for a minute. "Eh, well, as long as I don't have to pay for shit. And I'm not driving either."

"You don't have to. We have a party bus, fully stocked." Taj grinned.

"Woohoo! We need to celebrate." DJ Phatty headed for the door. "What you got in your fridge?"

"Dude!" Taj tried to stop him, but it was too late. He jogged after his friend into the hallway. "You're gonna make a mess!"

Skyler D stood still for a moment. He peered around the door and could hear Phatty and Taj trampling down the stairs. He turned back to Taj's computer and sat in his desk chair.

Then he pulled a flash drive from his pocket. He quickly inserted it into Taj's computer and then immediately ripped it back out.

He just managed to slip it back into his pocket before Taj jogged back into the bedroom. "Hey, before Phatty destroys my fridge, how about we go grab a drink at Schmitty's?"

"Uh, yeah, sure." Skyler D hopped up and followed Taj downstairs. They heard the sound of clinking glass and, in the kitchen, they saw Phatty's ass crack hanging out of the refrigerator.

"Okay, let's go, Phatty!" Taj yelled. As Phatty's sloppy face turned around, Taj threw him the key to the Lamborghini.

"Follow me in the Lambo. I can't leave that in my driveway! We're going to make a quick stop and drop that car off in the Bandido's parking lot, on the way to Schmitty's."

"Okay," Phatty mumbled through his overly stuffed mouth.

Taj and Skyler D inconspicuously pulled into the back of the Bandido's parking lot in Taj's car, with Phatty tailgating behind them in the Lamborghini.

Taj pointed at an empty parking space by the trash dumpsters, signaling Phatty to park. He stationed the car and turned off the engine.

Cautiously, Phatty climbed out of the fancy Lambo and switched to Taj's old car. The guys made a clean getaway without being seen.

Thirty minutes later, the friends knocked glasses and toasted their Vegas trip. They each sipped their drinks as their eyes roved over the females in the room.

Taj spotted a brunette standing at the far end of the bar. She was hot with big, pouty lips and a curvy figure.

Taj nodded his chin toward her. "Those lips. They're so familiar! Where have I seen her before?"

Skyler D snorted. "You don't know her. Nice try, man."

Then the bartender greeted the brunette. "Hi, Bonnie. Nice to see you."

"I do know her!" Taj told his friends. He jumped up from the table and headed to her end of the bar. "Bonnie?"

The pretty brunette looked up and then cringed. She tried to look away, but Taj knew she had seen him. "Hey, Bonnie! Do you remember me? It's Taj."

Bonnie looked him up and down and then squinted at him. "Taj? 'Tall, Dark and Sexy'?"

Taj rubbed the back of his neck. "Ah, yeah. That's me! I'm just not as buff as I usually am. My glands have been acting up. But my eyesight sure works. I spotted those lips of yours from a mile away. Are they real?"

Bonnie gave Taj a flat smile and then gestured to her drink. "Um, hey, can you watch this for a minute? I'll be right back."

"Sure, no problem. Take your time," Taj said.

Bonnie rushed off to the bathroom, relieved to see the small window there had not been painted shut. She looked at the dirty toilet in front of the small window and then back at the door. Then she shuddered and put one foot on the toilet seat, determined to escape.

"Shit!" Her foot slipped and dipped into the toilet bowl. Undeterred and refusing to return to the bar, Bonnie hoisted herself onto the windowsill and squeezed through. Her skirt hooked on a nail and caught her half in and half out of the window.

Back at the bar, DJ Phatty and Skyler D walked over to where Taj guarded Bonnie's drink. "Yo, why are you babysitting that drink? I'm sure I could find a good home for it."

"No, man. This is Bonnie's. She's this nice girl I met on

that online dating site I told you about. She just happened to be here. I think it's meant to be!"

"Yeah, right, bro. That chick is wayyyyyy out of your league," Skyler said as he chuckled.

"I actually think I have a shot with this one!" Taj fired back.

Outside, behind the bar, Bonnie's skirt ripped and dropped her out of the window and onto a pile of trash bags. She got up and ran down the alley at full speed.

Inside, DJ Phatty leaned on the bar and looked at Bonnie's abandoned drink again. "You sure? Well, Skyler and I are thinking about heading out."

"She's probably just fixing her makeup," Taj said. "I'll catch up with you guys later."

Skyler snickered. "I'd be surprised if she's still in the building."

"Bonnie was definitely giving you the look. You got this, bro. Maybe we'll catch up later." DJ Phatty slapped Taj on the back and then left with Skyler D.

Taj looked around the bar, happy in his assessment that Bonnie was the best-looking girl there. He spun on his barstool and waited patiently, but an hour passed.

The bartender finally noticed Taj still sitting there and came over. "So, how's the martini?"

"Well, it's actually not mine," Taj said. "I'm waiting for a friend who's in the bathroom. I hope she doesn't have the runs or something. She's been in there for a while."

The bartender gave Taj a pitying look but shrugged and went to check the ladies' bathroom. She came back and leaned against the bar in front of Taj.

"There's no one in there. Sorry, hun. I guess she slipped out on you."

Taj's shoulders slumped as he looked at Bonnie's lipstick

stain on the martini glass. "Really? Well, okay, thanks for letting me know."

Then he slid the glass in the bartender's direction and wandered sadly out the door.

CHAPTER TWELVE

ON THE RISE

As Taj walked to his car defeated, he pulled out his phone and looked at his Instagram feed. He scrolled through the flood of so-called models and clout-chasers, then came to Janet's latest post.

Her picture in front of the Leaning Tower of Pisa accentuated her natural beauty. It made Taj yearn for something deeper than the typical facade he was used to seeing online. He liked her post and commented with the praise-hands emoji.

When Taj began to slide his phone back into his pocket, he noticed a man approaching him politely. "Hey, you're Taj, right?"

Taj looked around hesitantly and then confessed, "Um, yeah, that's me. What's up?"

"Right on, I'm J.C." The man extended his arm. "I'm

a photographer and caught your set at the Playboy Mansion." A beam of joy overtook Taj's gloomy face as he shook the man's hand. "Yeah, your energy on stage was epic. You slayed it!"

J.C. took out his phone and showed Taj a picture of him DJing at the Playboy Mansion, arms up in the air with girls surrounding him. The scene was like a flock of seagulls after a piece of bread. His face expressed all the joy of a picture taken on a rollercoaster ride.

He continued to scroll from one picture to the next. "Wow, these are great! You have some good content here, definitely diggin' the angles."

"Yeah, I would love to get some more shots with you that you can use for your portfolio. Maybe we can work something out?"

"Well, what do you have in mind?" asked Taj.

"Here's some of my other work." He showed Taj some other photos. "Lifestyle photography is my main passion and recently I've been capturing a lot of DJs in the EDM scene. How 'bout in exchange for some photos, you get me into your next gig?"

Taj nodded. "Yeah, that sounds legit. Actually, I'm dropping a set tomorrow at an exclusive speakeasy. I can send you the details."

J.C. reached into his pocket and took out a business card. "Here, just take my card. I'll cruise through tomorrow night."

"Cool, I'll text you later," Taj responded. They shook hands and went in opposite directions.

Taj got into his car, then felt a vibration in his pocket. He checked his phone and saw a direct message from Janet. "Ciao, from Italy!"

Taj quickly replied: "I love the movie *Gladiator*! I've always wanted to visit the Colosseum in Rome!"

Janet followed up: "That's where I'm headed next, how did you know? :)"

"Awesome, I had no clue!" Taj typed.

His conversation with Janet was interrupted by a sharp bang on his car window...

A homeless man startled Taj, peering through his window and yelling, "I'll clean all your windows for a dollar!"

Taj nervously cracked his car window. "No, thank you, it's supposed to rain tomorrow."

The homeless man yelled back in an annoyed high pitch. "It's July, muthafucka!"

He then proceeded to spray Taj's window with a dirty liquid.

Taj failed to roll the window up in time and some of the mystery liquid splashed onto his face. "Ugh, that isn't window cleaner, it smells like piss!"

The man began wiping the window with an old pair of underwear. With every stroke the window got cloudier. Taj started up his car and peeled out.

"Where's my dollar at!?" the homeless man yelled, and then threw his spray bottle at the car, where it exploded on contact.

Taj sped down the street, got home, and headed straight to his bathroom sink. He vigorously scrubbed his face to remove the mystery liquid that landed on him.

Exhausted, he took everything out of his pockets and noticed J.C.'s business card.

The man's pictures were really good, so Taj sent him a text message: "What's up J.C.! So, the speakeasy is called the Quiet Room, password is 'be quiet.'"

Taj dropped the phone on his desk and plopped onto his bed to take a nap but slept through the night. Early the following morning, he opened his eyes to see his father, Prasad, standing over him.

"Your car smells like urine, Taj," Prasad said with a stern face.

"Huh, what are you talking about?" Taj asked, half awake.

"I went outside this morning to water the grass and the smell of piss was unbearable. The closer I got to your car the stronger the smell was. I sprayed it down with water already, but you should go dry it off."

Taj cringed. "I thought there was rain in the forecast."

Prasad walked toward the door, shaking his head. "It's July, you idiot."

Taj heard a notification coming from his phone. He picked it up to see a message from J.C.: "Is it cool to bring my camera tonight?"

"I'll make sure you're all good," Taj replied. J.C. quickly responded with a thumbs-up emoji.

Then, per the morning ritual, Taj checked his social media and was happy to see a message from Janet. "Hey Taj. Hope you're ok. :)"

Taj realized he didn't respond to a whole string of her messages after his encounter with the crazed homeless man. "I wish you were here with me," read the first message. Followed by another five minutes later: "That was stupid, sorry." Then two minutes after: "We don't even really know each other that well." Finally: "Have a good night, didn't mean to be weird."

"Oh man, she probably thinks I'm not into her now," he muttered out loud. Then he sent a quick reply. "Hey Janet :) I'm so sorry for not replying back last night! You wouldn't believe what happened."

Janet responded shortly after. "No worries Taj. I'm glad you're ok. We'll talk soon." She sent a picture of her standing in front of the Colosseum with her family.

"Amazing!" Taj quickly replied, then tried to make up for last night's gap in messages. "You're not stupid and the furthest thing from weird. I didn't mean to leave you hanging. Wish I was there too :)."

Taj waited, hopeful, but his messages didn't get read in time; Janet had already logged off. "Fuck!" Taj yelled, not caring it was a quiet morning.

He threw himself back onto the bed in exasperation. He stared at the old glow-in-the-dark stars on the ceiling and, as if responding to his current situation, one gently fell onto his chest.

Aashi happily burst into the room holding a freshly ironed shirt on a hanger. "Good morning, Taj. I bought you a new shirt to DJ in!"

Taj halfheartedly smiled at his mother. "Thank you, Mom. You know you didn't have to do that."

"Well, I want you to look sharp!" she said proudly. "You know, I think it's great that you're becoming a success in something you love to do. I know you're going to be a big star, and I'll always be your number-one fan—"

Aashi's sentence got cut short as she was overcome with a heavy cough. She took a seat at Taj's desk, gasping for air.

"Mom, are you okay?" Taj asked, jumping up in concern.

Aashi held up a hand. "I'll be okay, don't worry."

"You don't sound okay; your cough is sounding worse," replied Taj.

His mother finally caught her breath. "The doctor still has more tests to do, but I'm sure I'll be fine."

Taj sat in silence, wanting to believe her. Aashi leaned in. "Listen to me, Taj. No matter what happens, you have to keep going. It's your time to shine now."

Taj embraced his mother with a hug as warm as the sun beaming through a window.

"I'm going to make you proud, Mom. I can feel things are coming together," Taj announced with confidence.

Aashi stood up and walked slowly to the door before she glanced back at Taj with a smile.

"I'm already the proudest mother."

That night, Taj arrived at what looked like a small, run-down bookstore with a line of mostly guys waiting outside. There he spotted J.C. at the end of the line and signaled to him to follow him. "Hey, J.C., over here."

J.C. was excited to see Taj and followed him past the line. Taj confidently nodded to the security guard, who did not recognize him.

A giant hand stopped Taj and J.C. in their tracks. "Woah, woah, woah, the line starts over there." He jabbed a thick finger at the end of the line.

"Hey, bro, I'm the DJ, and this is my photographer," Taj announced.

The security guard looked down at his clipboard, his baseball glove-sized hand still extended. "Gimme your ID."

Taj pulled out his Dragon Ball Z wallet and handed over his driver's license with a crisp two-dollar bill under it. He then winked at the unimpressed security guard. The guard took his time finding Taj's name on the list with a plus-one.

Finally he returned Taj's license and moved aside. "Alright, Taj, welcome to the Quiet Room. Walk to the back and knock three times on the metal door."

"Cool, thanks!" replied Taj. He and J.C. entered in and walked toward the back of the unkempt store where they found the metal door.

Taj knocked three times and a slot opened, revealing a pair of large, staring eyes. "What's the password?" a heavy monotone voice asked.

"Be quiet." Taj was glad he remembered.

The slot closed abruptly. Taj stared at the door with a smile, anticipating a warm welcome. After a few seconds of nothingness, Taj turned to J.C. "It was 'be quiet,' right?"

Taj knocked again. Before the slot could fully open, Taj yelled, "Be quiet!" It immediately began to close again, and J.C. stuck his hand in to pry it open. He then let out a blood-curdling scream and yanked his hand back and lifted up his bloody index finger, staring in disbelief. "What the fuck? Someone bit me!?"

"Oh shit, dude, your nail is missing!" Taj exclaimed. He then banged angrily on the metal door. It swung open to reveal a tall, imposing figure wearing a tight dress. "Which one of you fucks stuck their finger in my slot?"

The intimidating stature of the person left Taj and J.C. speechless for a moment before Taj mustered up enough courage to stammer, "Uh, sorry about the confusion with the password, sir."

The doorperson quickly cut him off. "It's miss!"

"Of course, my mistake. I'm Taj, the DJ for tonight, and this is my guest." He pointed to J.C., sucking on his finger and grimacing in pain.

"Well, why didn't you say so?" the door person yelled.

"'Be quiet' was last week's password. This week it's 'inside voice.'"

"Okay, I'll be sure to take note of that!" Taj said, getting nervous.

The doorperson pointed to Taj's DJ bag. "What's in the bag, shorty?"

"Oh, it's my laptop," Taj explained.

"Alright, get inside. There's bandages at the bar." The door person moved aside and the dimly lit room came into view. The 20s-inspired bar was jam-packed with socialites and selfie-takers.

Taj and J.C. had to weave through camera flashes in order to reach the closest bartender.

The bartender lifted a glass lid and revealed a smoking drink. She passed it to a mesmerized customer and flicked her eyes over Taj. He slid the bartender two wrinkled drink tickets and pointed to the smoky drink. "Excuse me, miss, I'll have two of those as well." Taj tried his best smile on her. "Oh, and a Band-Aid, also."

J.C. wrapped a napkin around his finger while waiting. "Thanks, Taj. Man, I can't believe I almost lost my shooting finger. I'd totally be out of work."

"I know, right? That lady is crazy!" Taj exclaimed. J.C. glanced back at the doorperson, who stared intensely back while using his missing fingernail as a toothpick.

The bartender rushed back with two foamy beers in sample-size cups and a snooty attitude. "Your drink tickets are only good for domestic beer, and it's a no-go on the Band-Aids, hun."

The guys were not impressed but took their complimentary drinks anyway. Taj looked at the miniature cup and noticed lipstick on the rim.

He gave it a half turn before taking a sip. A look of disgust washed over his face. "Ugh, this beer is warm and flat! Is this how you treat the DJ?"

J.C. took a sip and immediately spit it back into the cup. The bartender laughed. "Yeah, right, you're a DJ?"

Before Taj could respond, the bartender turned to help another customer. Taj reached into his pocket and pulled out a wad of drink tickets, slamming them on the bar. "These are useless!"

Aggravated, Taj walked off into the crowd, J.C. quickly following. As they walked toward the packed dance floor, Taj spotted Elijah Wood DJing. "Hey, that's Frodo! Make sure to snap some shots."

"Yeah, sure." J.C. fumbled to focus the camera around his neck while Taj made his way closer to the stage. The crowd erupted as Elijah Wood shook a bottle of water in the air, wetting everyone around him. J.C. took cover behind Taj, protecting his camera.

"Aww shit!" J.C. panicked, but the splashing quickly ended.

Taj tapped Elijah Wood on the shoulder and lifted the headphone off his ear. "Hey, I think it's my turn to go on, Eli."

Elijah Wood turned his head with an angry frown and elbowed Taj back. "Watch out, li'l bitch! I got one more."

Taj stumbled back, crying, "Hey, Frodo, you're going into my time!"

Elijah Wood flipped him off and continued DJing. Taj glanced into the crowd and spotted a group of girls glaring at him, upset he was bothering Elijah Wood. J.C. was no help; he was busy talking to a girl and not paying attention to the altercation.

Taj took another step back only to get shoved from behind. "Hey, you fuckin' with my boy?"

He turned around, surprised to see actor Sean Astin fuming and ready to fight.

"Sam?" Taj blurted out, confused.

Sean Astin's eyes lit up with rage. "My name's not Sam, asshole!"

With his right hand, he backhanded Taj as a barrage of flashes went off. Taj touched his cheek in shock and looked over to see J.C. snapping photos.

Sean Astin taunted Taj. "You wanna take this outside or what?"

Taj lifted up his hands. "Dude, I'm a fan! I don't want beef."

Sean Astin cracked his knuckles. "That's what I thought, pussy!" He then front flipped off the stage.

Bewildered, Taj tried to focus by taking his laptop out of his bag and powering it on. In front, the crowd cheered for Elijah Wood, who grabbed the microphone: "Yo, Quiet Room, it's been real! Much love! Wooden Wisdom, out!"

Elijah Wood bumped into Taj on his way off the stage. On the dance floor, Wood was greeted by a beautiful model at least two feet taller than he was.

"My Precious, let's go smoke this joint."

Taj clambered quickly up on the stage and plugged a cord into his laptop and picked up the microphone. "Give it up one more time for Frodo, making it all the way out from Middle-earth! I'm Taj, the headliner, and this set is dedicated to all the ladies in the Quiet Room!" The Quiet Room finally lived up to its name. The awkward silence was only broken by Sean Astin yelling, "I'm gonna fuck you up!"

Taj pressed the spacebar and the music began. The heckling continued, but only the men booed. All the women in the speakeasy turned to Taj as if a magnet pulled their eyes and ears.

Ecstasy, excitement and energy overcame them. The party flooded onto the stage and a swarm of girls flew into a frenzy.

The addictive frequency blaring out of the speakers was irresistible to every woman there.

J.C. snapped photos, his mouth open in disbelief, while even Elijah Wood's girlfriend rushed toward the stage. Puzzled, he screamed over the music, "Hey, babe, where are you going?" She ignored him and continued in Taj's direction. She charged right up on stage and slipped behind Taj, aggressively tickling him and playfully mimicking his DJ moves.

"Hey, stop that!" Taj giggled. She kissed Taj on his neck as Elijah Wood stared in a jealous stupor.

Wood turned to Sean Astin. "Can you believe this shit!?"

"I know, his music is actually pretty dope!" Astin replied, bobbing his head to the beat.

Several girls had their phones pointed at the stage, ecstatic to take selfies with Taj dancing awkwardly in the background. Angry boyfriends couldn't call back their girlfriends' attention as they all clamored for Taj. Every one of them in the speakeasy moved and grooved, including the doorperson, who rhythmically tapped a foot.

Barely twenty minutes into Taj's set, a fire truck pulled up to the bookstore. A burly fire marshal jumped out, holding a megaphone.

He marched directly to the disheveled security guard. "How many people are inside?"

The security guard looked down at his clipboard, then his clicker, and finally at the fire marshal. "Uh..." He dropped everything and bolted down the street at a full-on sprint.

Taj DJed at the center of all the screaming attention, grinning before he spotted the fire marshal's angry entrance. The fire marshal looked over the crowd and barked through his megaphone, "Okay, sorry, folks, party's over!"

Taj reluctantly lowered the volume.

"Shut it down! You're over capacity!"

The music halted completely, and everyone stopped to stare at the fire marshal.

"Oh shit," Taj said into the microphone, and it echoed around the room.

The speakeasy's house lights turned on.

Taj fumbled the microphone, causing loud and excruciating feedback. "Uh, you heard the fireman, party's over."

Everyone from the speakeasy poured out onto the street. Taj lost sight of J.C. as he weaved through the crowd and out the door.

Outside, an old lady selling flowers held out a rose to Taj. "Para tu amor?"

Taj shook his head. "Sorry, I don't understand."

The lady smiled. "It's for your love."

He tried to laugh nonchalantly, but he thought of Janet. "Oh, I don't have a significant other, but hopefully someday I will."

A couple bumped Taj farther along the sidewalk as they staggered out of the bookstore. He looked around for J.C., but the photographer was nowhere to be found.

Not in the mood to search for him, Taj walked alone to his car. He didn't want to reflect on the night, so he pulled out his phone to scroll through Instagram. A new story from Janet appeared in his feed. She was on a gondola in Venice celebrating her birthday.

He sent her a balloon emoji and a message: "HBD gorgeous!" Then he glanced up and saw the couple that bumped into him making out under a streetlight. He sighed; loneliness was his only companion.

The next morning, Taj woke up to a bombardment of notifications. He rubbed the sleep out of his eyes and reached for his phone. He had ten missed calls from Phatty and a barrage of text messages: "Yo, you alive? Check your IG! Where you at? Call me back ASAP!"

Taj checked his Instagram and a flurry of mentions appeared on his activity tab. Wide-eyed, he scrolled through various pictures and video clips of last night's madness.

"Holy shit! This is lit!" Taj exclaimed, seeing some of the tags coming from J.C.'s account. The first post he checked had a caption that read: "Almost lost my shooting finger last night, but it was soooo worth it! One of the most insane evenings of my life! Shout-out to @tajthedj for inviting me to capture all the chaos!"

The comments on J.C.'s post read: "QTPI!" "OMG, that looks insane!" "I need to be at the next @tajthedj show!" "Does he need backup dancers?" "I was there!" "@tajthedj is such a hottie!" "J.C. is he single?"

Taj glanced over into his mirror and admired himself. "Who, me? Fuck yeah!"

He could not contain his enthusiasm, whooping as he continued to scroll through the mentions. A post from TMZ's account came up with the headline: "Elijah Wood Loses Girlfriend to Local DJ." Taj's jaw dropped.

Before he could read the article, his agent Lance called. "Yo, Lance, what's up?"

"Hey, Taj! Great news, I just spoke with Jimmy Fallon's people and they want you to be a guest on the show!"

Taj looked at his phone in disbelief.

"Whhhhaaaatttt!? That's amazing news!"

"Yeah, Taj, you got some buzz going. Jimmy and his producers saw the clips of you stealing Elijah Wood's girl at your show. Ha, you're a real ladies' man! They're eager to have you on."

"I can't believe it!" exclaimed Taj.

"Yes, it's going to be a great promo for your Vegas gig as well. Mark your calendar, you'll be on Thursday before you play at XS!" Lance said.

"Nice! Can't wait to tell my parents about this!" Taj said gleefully.

Lance replied, "We're going to let everyone know by tomorrow! I'll send over the promos for you to post in a bit."

"Sounds good, thanks!"

"I have to make some calls, I'll talk to you later, Taj!"

Taj put the phone back on the nightstand and sat in stunned silence for a few seconds. He looked at his reflection in the mirror again and then jumped up with a huge smile.

"I'm going to be on the muthafuckin' *Tonight Show*! Wooooooooo!" With his arms high in the air, Taj ran around his room yelling: "Ji-mmy Fa-llon, Ji-mmy Fa-llon!"

Prasad marched into Taj's room at that moment. "What's all the commotion about?"

Taj responded with excited pride. "My agent just called to tell me I'm going to be on the *Tonight Show*!"

Prasad's stern face relaxed. "The one with Jimmy Fallon?"

"Yes!"

"Oh I like him! Not a great actor, but he's good on the show," Prasad replied with a slight smile.

"I have to tell Mom!" Taj jetted out of his room and headed downstairs to tell Aashi the news.

Prasad's smile did not last. He looked down and picked up the glow-in-the-dark star that had fallen from the ceiling. As he stood alone staring at the sticker, a disconcerted look came over his face and he reminded himself out loud: "My son can do better than DJing."

CHAPTER THIRTEEN

NEW YORK TO VEGAS

Aashi shuffled into the dining room with the newspaper under her arm. "Sorry, dear, but the rest of the patisa is gone."

Prasad snorted. "Taj's friends were here again. I wish he would keep that pudgy one away from our refrigerator."

"Speaking of Taj..." Aashi pulled up a chair next to her husband, opened the newspaper and lovingly smoothed it out. "Look, Prasad. Our son is in the newspaper! They say he's the next DJ to 'blow up.' What does that mean?"

Taj's father reluctantly looked at the newspaper article and grainy photograph. He pursed his lips at his son's ridiculous outfit and then scanned the first few lines. "Well, I guess that means people like him."

"Oh! Good for him." Aashi eased back in her chair and smiled.

Her husband could not mirror her contented look. "Yes, but is this the future you want for your son? What about when the next big DJ comes along? Then Taj will be back working at the store."

Aashi didn't want to argue, so she focused on the photograph of her son. It made her smile. "If this is what he loves doing, then we need to let him."

Prasad grunted and pushed back from the table, but all it took was his wife to lay one gentle hand on his arm for him to stop.

"Remember your dreams of being an actor?" Aashi asked her husband. "You were so ambitious."

"I think you mean foolish," Prasad said.

"Or maybe I meant happy. Don't you remember?"

Taj's father gave a small nod, the slightest shadow of a smile appearing at the corners of his mouth. "I found other ways to be happy. We had a family."

Aashi smiled, glad her husband was slowly coming around. "Taj doesn't have any children yet, and this is the land of opportunity. He's passionate about music and we have to be there to support him."

Prasad kissed her cheek and nodded again, though he would say nothing more on the matter. He was still waiting to see exactly what became of his son's so-called music.

Taj blew up, but it didn't feel like an explosion. It felt like a speeding car with all sorts of clubs, crowds and successes flashing by him at high speed. No one could go online or turn on the television without some mention of him popping up. The news of Taj's fame was quickly spreading, and his name was trending all over the Internet. With his new celebrity status, more girls were interested in him, even without his music playing.

Aashi was so proud, and the refrigerator was soon covered in magazine and newspaper clippings. She had Prasad print articles so she could add them to her collection. But she worried about Taj; he barely had time to eat, and from what she had observed, all he did was party and play music.

"Don't worry, Mother, I eat at five-star restaurants," Taj had assured her during one of their occasional phone conversations.

"You can, or you do?" Aashi tried not to worry, but her son did not call her enough, and he hardly had any time to be at home.

In New York, Taj leaned back and lounged on the sofa as he related that sweet story to Jimmy Fallon. The crowd gave a heartfelt "aww" in response, and the popular late-night talk-show host grinned. "Hello, Taj's mom! Don't worry, there's plenty of food in our green room."

Taj checked his slicked-back hair. He was sweating under the stage lights, but he refused to take off his expensive leather jacket or his dark sunglasses. Instead he gave the camera and his faraway mother a casual wave.

"So, Taj, what makes you the hottest DJ on the scene right now? I mean, the ladies are flocking to your shows," Jimmy said.

Taj tipped his dark sunglasses and gave the camera a wink. "Well, Jimmy, I basically just drop my beats and all the girls in the club have a major eargasm!"

"An eargasm?" the late-night talk show host repeated.

"Yeah, you know, it's like an orgasm, but in your ear." The

audience whistled and cheered. Taj stood up and pumped up the audience even more.

"Can you dig ittttt?"

They went wild and it took a few moments before everyone settled down enough for Jimmy's next question: "So, I hear you have a big show in Vegas this weekend?"

Taj flopped back down on the couch and stopped mugging for the audience long enough to grin at Jimmy and say, "Yeah, that's right! I'm making my Sin City debut with Tiesto at Club XS!"

The band did their best rendition of Tiesto's "Adagio for Strings," but the audience was screaming so loud it could barely be heard. Taj jumped up and waved the audience onto their feet. Soon the whole set was bumping. Jimmy ran out from behind his desk and made everyone laugh with his best dance moves.

When the music stopped and the audience settled down, Jimmy nudged Taj with his elbow. "So, hey, yeah, um, you think you could get me backstage?"

Laughter rang out again as Jimmy tried to act cool.

Finally, Taj gave him a pat on the shoulder. "My guest list is kinda full, Jimmy... but I'll see what I can do."

The talk-show host crossed his fingers for the crowd and then retreated back behind his desk. Taj settled back down onto the couch and tipped down his dark sunglasses again as he smiled directly into the camera. It zoomed in close on his face.

"By the way, make sure to check out my website at: ladies-love-Taj-dot-com!"

"Is that where we can find some of your music?" Jimmy asked.

"Well, I don't release my tracks online, Jimmy. If people

want to experience the magic of my beats, they have to come out to my shows!"

He understood that releasing his music to the public meant that chaos would ensue. The risk was too great to have his beats played outside of his control.

"Well, I know I speak for everyone when I say we hope to get music from you soon!" Jimmy said excitedly. Taj gave a smile and shrugged. "Am I right, everyone?" Jimmy looked at the audience as they all cheered in agreement. "Alright, Taj, thanks for coming on the show!"

Taj shook the talk-show host's hand. "Thank you, Jimmy, it was lit."

From there, Taj sent flirty smiles into the audience as Jimmy introduced the next guest.

"When we come back, just released from his tenth stint in rehab—Justin Bieber!"

Phatty sat on his front steps like an oversized kid waiting to go to summer camp. A lumpy duffel bag sat next to him, but he moved it when Skyler D paced by.

"Sit down. I'm sure Taj will be here soon," Phatty called.

"He better not have forgotten," Skyler D muttered. He refused to sit on the step and instead stomped up and down the front sidewalk again. "Unless he made the whole thing up."

The thought cheered Skyler D up marginally, until he cringed at how easy it was to hate his friend for his success. All anyone talked about anymore was Taj. Even Phatty mentioned Taj more than he talked about snacks.

Skyler D dragged himself to the steps and finally sat down next to Phatty. "You really believe his beats have some sort of magic frequency?"

"We're about to find out!" Phatty jumped up and almost left without his duffel bag. "Come on, I see the party bus!"

The party bus pulled up to the curb and the bass rattled the windows of Phatty's house. He hopped eagerly from one foot to the other as the door finally burst open in a flood of laser lights, loud music and feminine squeals. Phatty's eyes went wide, and he stood in front of the blue runner lights with his mouth hanging open.

"Come on. Let's go!" Skyler D pushed past his friend and jumped onto the bus.

Phatty's mouth gaped wider as he followed Skyler D. The driver, an unimpressed man roughly the size of a small mountain, nodded at them.

"How does he keep his eyes on the road?" Phatty asked Skyler D.

Skyler D shrugged, speechless. In front of them four women danced around a pole wearing nothing but G-strings. Their tiny scraps of dresses were strewn over the side benches as if they had just been flung off. In fact, the women danced with such wild abandon that it was clear they were enjoying themselves and not just jiggling around in sexy high heels for money.

The women laughed and threw their hands in the air as another of Taj's songs pumped through the party bus speakers. Hips thrusted to the beats, breasts bounced, and one enthusiastic dancer began peeling off her little satin thong. She tossed it over her head with a wild laugh and it landed on Phatty's stomach.

He plucked it up with shaky fingers. "Um, hi."

Phatty's voice cracked, and his chubby cheeks blushed bright red. The now completely naked woman snatched back her thong and gave him a pitying smile.

"Wow, you're so pretty." Phatty sighed.

"Yeah, buddy, we got five hours in this bitch!" Taj yelled from the back of the bus.

They found Taj sprawled out across the back seat with sunglasses on. He waved at them with a bottle of champagne in his hand, his other hand around the shapely waist of another almost-naked woman.

She pressed against him and bounced gently to the beat while tousling his slicked-back hair.

"See?" Taj tipped down his dark sunglasses and waggled his eyebrows at his friends. "I told you! They can't get enough of my beats!"

Phatty responded with his best dance moves and the party bus swayed, but that didn't stop him. Taj's mood was contagious. The women kept dancing despite Phatty's flailing arms, and the only person besides the stoic driver not moving to the music was Skyler D. He took a casual seat but couldn't keep his eyes from roaming enviously from one end of the bus to the other.

The woman sitting on Taj's lap reached behind him and dug out a tiny see-through purse that held nothing but a key and a small bag of blow. She dipped the key into the powder and then thoughtfully tapped it onto her taut nipple. Taj leaned forward and sniffed it up with a satisfied grin.

"Ahhhhh!"

"Woohoo! Sin City, here we come!" Phatty yelled out.

Skyler D shook his head and moved farther away from his accident-prone friend. Soon, the bus was on the highway and three more bottles of champagne had been popped. Even though he couldn't believe his own eyes, he finally started to relax.

"So, hey! I'm Skyler D. How do you know Taj?" he asked the leggy redhead in front of him.

She paused in her dancing long enough to crinkle her nose at him in confusion. "Doesn't everyone know Taj?"

She went back to dancing without noticing that Skyler D had poured her a plastic glass of champagne. Everyone was drinking straight from their own bottles anyway. The bus hit a pothole in the road and Skyler's drink splashed all over him. He slumped back in his seat and shook his head.

"This can't be happening," he muttered.

Even more concerning than being shot down so soon was the fact that Taj was a hit with the ladies. He sat on the back seat like a throne but often got up to join the ladies on the dance floor where he did nothing more than let them all rub up and down against him. The women were mesmerized by his rhythmless dance moves.

Taj turned to one of the women and gave her a long, sloppy and very lip-smacking kiss.

The women couldn't get enough of him, and throughout the ride he took turns kissing them all.

Secretly, Taj pretended they were all the same woman. Maybe even his girlfriend.

Miles away, Janet was snuggled up on her couch reading a book. After reading the same page three times, she put down her book and picked up her phone.

She texted Taj: "Hi cutie :) Just got back last night. What ya doing?"

Taj was so busy making the rounds of ladies on the party bus that he never heard his phone buzz. It was the special, sweet little hook that he'd put on his phone just for Janet.

Back in the regular world, Janet fixed lunch in her tiny apartment kitchen and forced herself to eat at a normal pace, finishing the whole plate before she allowed herself to check her phone again.

No text message.

Janet was sad Taj didn't respond. She had felt something special when they met. She thought he had too. Now she just felt silly for reaching out. In order to make herself feel better, Janet logged on to Facebook and changed her status to "In a Relationship." Then she put her phone down and picked up her book again.

Taj sped farther and farther away, completely caught up in the commotion of the party bus and the new crazy trajectory of his life.

CHAPTER FOURTEEN

WYNN BIG

The only thing the party bus driver said the entire trip was: "Entering city limits. Welcome to Las Vegas."

Bright sunlight streamed into the party bus, blinding the dancers and their admirers. Taj laughed and chortled, still wearing his dark sunglasses. Skyler D covered his eyes and stumbled over the redhead. She didn't even notice him crash across the dance floor to the opposite side bench.

The music continued to play and the women kept dancing. And no one on the Vegas Strip seemed surprised to see a party bus full of naked ladies dancing in broad daylight.

Phatty blinked and squinted, too excited to see the Strip to let his eyes adjust. He waved at the crowds of people milling up and down in front of the gargantuan casinos.

Then he popped up with an excited yelp. "Whoa! Taj,

you're on that billboard with Tiesto!"

Taj scrambled out of his seat, knocking two of the girls out of the way. He ripped off his sunglasses and peered out the window in the direction Phatty pointed. "No way. Where? Where!?"

The billboard grew in size as they approached it, and soon Taj's image was towering over them. The party bus driver drove on without slowing, completely unimpressed. Skyler limped over just in time before it passed them by.

He laughed. "Where did they get that picture from?"

Skyler pointed out Taj's bright-green Crocs and then pretended to cower as the giant green shoe loomed over the top of the bus.

Phatty laughed too. The oversized version of Taj's bad taste was funny enough to tear his glance away from the still-dancing women.

"Did you see that?" Taj hopped up and down. "It was promoting our show. I'm really going to be on the same stage as Tiesto!"

"You sure?" Skyler D asked. "He and the rest of the Strip might get one look at those Crocs and call off the show."

Taj didn't hear him at all.

The music was still pumping through the party bus speakers, and when he stood up, the women surrounded him.

"Holy shit, there I am! The king is here!" Taj shouted.

He broke into a victory dance, something similar to a flapping chicken being bounced like a basketball. The women squealed with delight and followed his every move.

Skyler D sat back and shook his head. "I can't believe what I'm seeing right now."

"Neither can I." Phatty licked his lips and pressed his nose to the bus window. "No way, Aria has a new buffet?"

They cruised the rest of the Strip with Taj leading his ladies around and around the pole in a wild conga line while Phatty's belly undulated to the beat of his hungry stomach.

Skyler D was relieved when the party bus finally pulled into the Wynn Hotel. He jumped up and yelled, "We're here!"

He was the first down the bus steps and jumped out so fast he almost knocked over the hotel employee who was waiting politely outside. Phatty followed and gave the surprised employee a sympathetic smile.

Behind him the women bounced out, just barely back into their skin-tight dresses.

The hotel employee raised his voice to be heard over Taj's loud music. "Welcome to the Wynn! Can I help you with your luggage?"

Phatty followed the employee's eyes from the women down to his lumpy duffel bag. "Thanks, but I think we've got it from here."

Taj appeared on the bus steps, and the second his feet hit the ground the party bus driver turned off the music. He turned quickly to the confused women and waved his hand at them.

"Okay, ladies. Thanks! Get lost!"

Phatty did not notice their bewildered looks as he waved at the women one last time. "It was nice to meet you."

The hotel employee cleared his throat and tried his welcome speech again, but he was interrupted by Taj's phone ringing. Taj searched every pocket, then his bag, and then his pockets again before his phone somehow fell out of his shirt.

The poor employee only had time to shove room keys into Phatty's hands. He quickly listed the room numbers before Taj answered his phone and cut him off.

"It's my agent. I've got to get this," Taj said.

Skyler D rolled his eyes and took the room keys from Phatty. "And we'll get him to his room."

Phatty nodded. "Maybe there'll be time for some room service."

"Hey, Lance. What's up?" Taj strode across the white marble floor of the lobby; he only had to be redirected twice by Skyler D.

"Hi, Taj. Are you here yet?" Lance asked.

Taj was confused as they walked through the casino. The jangling slot machines gave way to roulette tables and the green-felted semicircles of blackjack.

Even the bright red swirls of the intense carpet were disorienting. He wandered off down a video poker aisle, but Phatty caught his arm and dragged him back.

Luckily, his friends assured him they were heading to his hotel room as Taj nodded. "Yup. I just got to the hotel."

Skyler D and Phatty yanked Taj into the elevator before he wandered off again, and they rode up listening to him describe the party bus trip in all its glory to Lance.

"Buses will never be my first choice, but it sounds like it was great. I'll see you for dinner at eight?" Lance asked.

"Sounds good, see you then!" Taj finally finished up the chat with his agent as they came up to the first of their hotel room doors. He hung up his phone and then snatched the room keys out of Skyler D's hands.

"Alright, guys, I got two rooms right by each other. One for both of you and one for me."

Skyler D pushed past Taj so he would be the first one in the room but he stopped, and both his friends ran right into him. "This is it?" he asked incredulously. "There's only one fucking bed!"

Taj shrugged his shoulders. "I guess this is all they had."

It was a standard hotel room with one king-size bed and no amenities. Phatty sucked in his stomach and squeezed past Skyler D before tossing his duffel bag on the bed. He sat down on the end and bounced happily.

"Comfy, feels like memory foam," Phatty said with a smile. "Hey, but there's only one pillow?"

"Don't worry about it, Phatty, you'll be sleeping in the bathtub. I need this bed for all the bitches I'll be pulling," Skyler D said with a smirk.

Phatty bounced up and gave Taj a light punch on the shoulder. "Whatever. This is perfect. Thanks, bro!"

Taj returned his punch with a hard-slapping high five. "No worries, I'm just glad you guys made it out for my big show."

He did his awkward chicken victory dance back to the hotel room door and was surprised when both his friends followed him.

"Do you know the Wi-Fi password?" Phatty asked. "I told my mom I'd Skype with her later."

Skyler eyed the room key in Taj's hand. "What's your room like?"

"Well, uh." Taj cleared his throat. "I got an upgrade from my agent."

Skyler D swiped the room key back from Taj and strode to the next door down the hall. "Let me guess, you asked for one with a heart-shaped bathtub or something."

"No, but—" Taj fluttered around but it was too late.

Skyler D threw the hotel room door wide open and then stood dumbfounded. Luxury suite was more accurate for the lavish display in front of him.

All the best amenities, plus a breathtaking panoramic view, had Taj's eyes going wide as he pushed past Skyler D and entered his hotel suite. "Now this is what I'm talking about," Taj said.

Beside the full-sized dining room table was a fully stocked bar, and Phatty made a beeline straight for it. He plucked the champagne bottle that had been left on ice and popped it open enthusiastically, perhaps too much so. The sparkling wine fizzed up and out of the bottle and Phatty's only idea to stop it was to plug it into his mouth. He gulped and coughed and had to drink more before he could even toast Taj.

Skyler D stood in the doorway, shaking his head. "Is that a one-lane bowling alley?"

"Holy shit, dude. It is!" Taj ran over and then squealed with delight as he spotted more to his luxury suite. "And there's a half-court with a full-sized basketball hoop!"

Taj was terrible at both games but was nonetheless excited at the extravagance of his suite.

At the bar, Phatty found a second bottle of champagne. He managed to open it less dramatically and actually pour it into tall crystal flutes.

Skyler D reluctantly joined them for the toast, though his eyes were too busy sweeping jealously over Taj's accommodations to actually clink his glass with his friends.

"Vivo Las Vegas!" Phatty mispronounced.

"You mean 'viva,'" Skyler D said.

"What?"

Skyler D sighed and finished his drink in one long gulp. "Never mind."

Taj sloshed his champagne as he hoisted his crystal flute high in the air. "Who cares? Here's to me! The king has arrived, Vegas. Are you ready!?"

"Nope." "Yup." Phatty and Skyler D spoke at the same time, but Taj didn't hear them.

He was too busy surveying his new kingdom as the sun set and the bright lights of the Strip blazed far up into the sky.

CHAPTER FIFTEEN

IN XS

Taj got lost on his way to the elevator and then again in the Wynn Hotel's lobby, but it felt good to be on his own. Now he knew what it was like to be famous: celebrity status was a buoy, and his old friends were weighing him down.

Skyler D had stalked off from his room earlier and was probably whining somewhere at a blackjack table. Phatty was nested happily in their little shared room with a whole cart of room service and the Wi-Fi password. Taj tried not to think of them as he dodged through the crowds and chaotic casino.

"Excuse me. Could you tell me where the Bruce Lee is?" Taj asked an overworked cocktail waitress.

She sighed at him, out of patience. "You mean the Wing Lei?"

Taj followed the jerk of her chin and saw the restaurant's large glowing sign. "Great, thanks."

The cocktail waitress was gone when Taj turned around and Lance was already calling him over. "Taj! Our table's ready."

Taj trotted after Lance to a table near the restaurant's towering golden dragon. "Hey, is it cool if I use a fork? I'm not much of a chopstick guy."

Lance ignored him and steered the conversation straight into business. "So, your set is from midnight to 1am. I reserved a VIP table for you with bottle service. Try not to drink too much, though. We want to make a good impression here."

Taj slumped in his seat and rolled his eyes. "Don't you worry about that. This is what I do!"

He scrambled to sit up straight, practically at attention as their very attractive waitress approached. So much for the casual and rebellious image. Taj even ratcheted his spine up an inch or two to be at eye level with her enormous fake breasts.

She waited patiently for his eyes to rise but didn't miss a beat when they stayed fixed on her chest. The big tips she always got had paid off the plastic surgery long ago. "Good evening, gentlemen. I'm Alice and I'll be your waitress for the evening. Can I get you guys started on some drinks?"

"Hey there, Alice. Has anyone ever told you you have a striking resemblance to Jennifer Lawrence?" Taj gave her his best grin.

Alice, who looked nothing like the famous actress, frowned. "Uh, no, sir. That's the first—"

Taj cut her off eagerly. "Probably because you're so much prettier than her!"

The waitress swallowed her distaste for terrible pickup lines and forced her smile to stay in place. "Thank you, sir."

Taj abandoned his posture again and tried to lean back casually despite the restaurant chairs being high-backed wood and stiff gold brocade. "Well, if you're not busy later tonight, I'll be DJing. You should come party!"

"Um, no." Alice brightened her smile. "I don't do clubs, but thanks for the invite. Are you gentlemen ready to order or do you need a few more minutes?"

Lance, who had been checking his phone for the entire exchange, looked up and was surprised to see the waitress there. "Yeah, we're going to need a few more minutes. Thanks, hun."

"No problem, sir," Alice said.

Taj scoffed. "Her loss! She probably has to work the late-night shift at Treasure Island."

Lance looked up from his phone and laughed because Taj laughed. "Don't worry. I'll order for the table."

Taj nodded, feeling like it was star treatment. "And tell her to bring me a fork."

He decided he should check his phone like Lance was doing again. He slipped the device out of his pocket but kept it under the table. Taj noticed Janet's text from earlier in the day but hesitated to respond.

Rising stars don't fall in love and settle down. At the same time, he noticed something had changed significantly on her Facebook status.

"Ah, what, she has a boyfriend now!?" His reaction contradicted the rising star's bravado. He tossed his phone on the table and startled Lance into responding to what he'd said.

"I guess she hasn't seen you rock a party, am I right?"

Lance chuckled while still scrolling through his messages. Taj decided Lance was right. He would figure out the whole Janet thing later when he could think. Right now he had to do Vegas, Taj style.

Taj gripped his laptop bag tighter as they started to pass the crowd outside of XS Nightclub. People behind the velvet rope snapped selfies and squealed in anticipation.

A few people recognized Taj and began snapping photos as he and his friends approached the doors.

"But don't I look good?" one woman whined at the bouncers. She shimmied her short skirt higher. "I'm telling you, Taj is not going to want to miss this."

Skyler D adjusted the collar of his designer suit. "What do you think? Should I help her out?" he asked Phatty and Taj.

Taj laughed, but it was too high-pitched, and he pursed his lips before any more of the nervousness escaped. The crowd noticed him as excitement filled the air.

A tall man in a shiny suit waved a thick fan of cash at the bouncers. "Hey, man. All this is yours if you just open up that rope."

They didn't even blink.

"Maybe we should have gone around back," Phatty said.

"No way. We look good. We've got to be seen," Skyler D said.

Taj played it cool and walked straight up to the bouncers. He cleared his throat loudly and made his presence felt. "Yo what's up. I'm Taj."

The bouncers turned and their frowns quickly changed into welcoming smiles. The taller bouncer noticed Taj's green Crocs. He nodded and the velvet rope opened wide.

Taj bounced inside XS with Phatty beaming and Skyler D a few steps behind them. Strobe lights, lasers and heavy bass blanketed the nightclub in hot-flashing anticipation. Taj tugged open his collar and spun around in a full circle as a gaggle of gorgeous women went by. A giant ornate disco ball spun under the XS chandelier, and the dizzying lights swept across the semicircle of private booths that faced the dance floor.

Pyrotechnics sparked on the corners of the stage and the crowd on the dance floor shrieked with excitement. Temporarily blinded, Taj tripped into a tall cocktail waitress delivering bottle service. She caught the expensive vodka before it crashed to the dance floor and sidestepped Taj before he could apologize.

He turned to follow her and ran into his agent.

Lance smoothed down his own suit and gave his client a brilliant smile. "Taj, glad you made it on time!"

Phatty grabbed the agent's hand and pumped it up and down in an energetic handshake. "Thanks! Thank you! This is so cool!"

Perplexed, Lance yanked back his hand but kept his smile in place. "Yeah, nice to meet you fellas."

He looked over to Skyler D and gave him a flirtatious wink. "Taj, who is *this!?*" Lance said flirtatiously.

Skyler D tried to avoid direct eye contact.

"Oh, who? Skyler?" Taj answered for him. "Yeah, he's one of my best buds and a great DJ."

"I love the name Skyler! It's so summery and unique. Let's exchange contact info later."

"Uh, sure," Skyler said hesitantly.

Lance motioned to a VIP booth. Taj ran over to the posh booth and jumped up and down on the alligator-skin cushions. Then he grabbed up the little gold-embossed sign and flashed his name in his friends' faces before holding it up high over his head. "Awesome! This is going to be an epic night!"

"We have a lot of presale tickets already sold, so epic is entirely possible," Lance said.

Skyler D was not ready to settle into a booth where ladies couldn't see him, but Phatty pushed him in. He had to be content with looking cool while perusing the assorted bottles of alcohol and juice in the center of the table.

"Compliments of the club," Lance pointed out.

"My man!" Taj was too excited to sit down.

"Dude, this is baller status," Phatty squealed.

Lance flagged down a short-haired blonde and wrapped his arm around her waist as he introduced her to the table. "This is your hostess, Samantha, and she'll get whatever you guys need."

Samantha grinned as she adjusted her midriff top, then smoothed her hands over her tight black shorts and fishnet stockings. The longer she lets the guys' gazes linger, the bigger the tip she figured she'd get.

"Hi. I'm DJ Skyler D."

"Who?" Samantha's smile slipped, then she turned to Taj. "You're the DJ opening tonight! O-M-G, can I get a picture with you!? My friends are not gonna believe I met Taj!"

Taj grinned ear to ear and popped up the itchy collar on his designer suit. "Sure, I don't see why not. Skyler, can you take a picture for Samantha?"

Skyler D scowled but took the hostess's phone. He held

it up as Taj awkwardly laced his arm around Samantha's bare waist. Then Skyler switched the camera to selfie mode.

"Okay, say cheese!" he called out as he took a picture of himself. Then Skyler D tossed the phone back to Samantha and poured himself a large drink.

"Excuse me, miss. Do you serve appetizers?" Phatty asked.

Samantha tucked her phone away in her impossibly short shorts and shook her blonde head.

"No, I'm sorry. We don't serve food."

Phatty gave her an understanding smile and then reached into his designer suit pocket. He pulled out a half-eaten chocolate bar and took a messy bite before saying, "Always gotta be prepared!"

Lance tried to stay focused on his client. "Come on, Taj. Your set is about to start. Let's head over to the DJ booth and get you dialed in."

Taj almost fell over trying to do a cool spin. "Alright, fellas, wish me luck!"

Samantha clapped her hands excitedly and Phatty gave him a smeary grin. "Dude, you're gonna kill it tonight!" he told Taj.

"Break a leg... or two," Skyler D muttered.

Phatty leaned back in the VIP booth and heaved a contented sigh. "This is the life right here! I hope my career takes off just like Taj's!"

Skyler D glanced around the packed club, his mood plummeting as he overheard excited people talking about Taj's "amazing" music.

He sneered at Phatty. "First you gotta lose some weight. The stage might collapse during your set!"

"Dude, why are you being so fucking negative?" Phatty frowned and sucked in his stomach.

"What?" Skyler D said. "I can't hear you over all these bullshit people. What do they know about good music?"

Phatty balled his chubby hands into fists and hammered his point on the table. "We're in Vegas, living it up, and you're about to watch our friend rock the biggest party of his life. Stop hating!"

Skyler D rolled his eyes and shoved Phatty's fists away from the expensive bottle of vodka. "Meh. I'm not hating."

"Yeah, right." Phatty gave his friend a sharp look. "You're just mad 'cuz Taj is doing it big and he finally has girls on his jock. He's performing at bigger shows than you and you're jealous. Admit it!"

"Shut the fuck up, DJ Fat Ass!" Skyler D punched Phatty on the shoulder. "You're just acting up 'cuz they don't serve food in here."

"Dude, whatever." Phatty's fierceness was ruined by an audible stomach growl that rumbled during the break of the beat.

CHAPTER SIXTEEN

TAJ SOLO

Taj walked onto the stage too soon and stumbled when the spotlight didn't illuminate his entrance. The house DJ wasn't quite done with his set or the lead-up hype, and Taj tried to play it cool while he stood out of place.

He tapped his feet in his clunky green Crocs and would have started dancing, except he had the nervous feeling of needing to pee.

The house music hit another silence, meant to call more attention to the stage and Taj took another confident step forward. Music blared again and he froze like a one-man game of red light/green light. Taj looked even stranger now that he stuck partially into the spotlight. The DJ caught sight of him and frowned.

He peeled back one of his headphones. "You lost, man?"

Taj laughed and trotted the rest of the way to the turn-tables. "No. I'm Taj!"

The house DJ looked unconvinced until Lance flagged him down in the affirmative from the wings. "Right on. Let's get this crowd going!"

A brief silence filled the nightclub as the two DJs shook hands and the crowd tried to figure out if it was time to be excited or not. The house DJ made room for Taj who scrambled to turn on his laptop and cue up his music.

"Come on, Taj. Time to let the magic begin!" he muttered to himself.

The crowd was quiet and skeptical until Taj turned on his first track at low volume. Even the intro was enough to get people screaming with excitement. More people flooded onto the dance floor, mostly women who shuddered with eagerness.

Feeling more confident now that his beats were backing him up, Taj grabbed the microphone. "XS, my name's Taj and I wanna know if Sin City is ready to get wavy!"

The nightclub erupted with cheers.

Taj spit all over the microphone as he shouted, "I said, who came to get lit?"

Tank tops were already coming loose, straps slipping down as women heated up.

They screamed and hemlines surged higher. Taj's music penetrated the club speakers and started to arouse the women to even more excited cheers.

"Then let's get this party poppin'!"

Taj's mouth was too close to the microphone and he sent a shriek of feedback through the club, but the turned-on crowd didn't notice.

The pyrotechnics spat fire in long blazing columns up to

the ceiling. All the ladies pushed straight to the front and clung to the stage in hopes of touching Taj. Bottle service had come to a halt as the XS bottle girls were also on the dance floor, enchanted by the beats. When the flames died out bright, sparkling confetti fell from the ceiling over the crowd.

Taj looked up at the crowd only to have a silky pair of panties fall on his face. He plucked them off with an ear-to-ear grin and pumped his fist in the air while the crowd swelled and screamed.

Even Phatty and Skyler D were on their feet, joining the crowd just outside their VIP booth. Sparkly confetti clung to Skyler D's gelled hair, and he picked it out while everyone else danced. He accidentally flung it on a nearby gorgeous girl and decided an apology would be the perfect pickup line.

"Sorry, sexy. I'm Skyler D. What's going on?" He leaned in and spoke into her ear.

The girl pushed his face away without even looking. She couldn't tear her eyes off Taj and blindly shoved forward in the hopes of touching him. Skyler D stood slack-jawed, unable to believe she wouldn't turn around.

"I said, what's going on?" Skyler D glared at her and then up at Taj. "I'm headed back to the room!"

Phatty was dancing unnoticed behind a heavyset woman and didn't look up until Skyler D swatted his arm. "Huh? What? You're leaving? Taj just started!"

"Fuck this," Skyler D spat. "I've seen enough."

"Dude, stop being such a downer!" Phatty's eyes bulged as the woman in front of him peeled off her shirt. "Can't you just have a good time?"

"How can you call this a good time?" Skyler D countered.

Phatty licked his lips and nodded to a horoscope tattoo on the woman's exposed back. "Look, this girl's a Gemini, that means we're compatible! At least give me a few minutes."

Skyler D grabbed Phatty by his thick arm. "Come on!"

"Ow, what the fuck?"

"I said, let's go, Phatty!"

Phatty's shoulders slumped. He had to admit that none of the women were noticing him. Still, he smiled up at Taj before reluctantly pushing through the crowd after Skyler D.

"Can we at least get a midnight snack?" he cried. "I'm starving."

Taj continued to rock the nightclub. The floor was so jam-packed that he couldn't see his friends. "At least they can see me," Taj told himself.

As he transitioned into the next beat, Taj pulled out his phone and turned his back on the crowd. He held it up high and snapped a selfie before sending it to Janet with a misspelled text message. Taj hoped she could tell what a wild success he was even though his selfie was awkwardly askew.

Taj snapped a few more pictures of the crowd, hoping to catch Phatty doing his signature dance moves, but all he saw was topless women.

Not that Taj was complaining; he grinned and slipped his phone back into his pocket.

The rest of the set was a blur of breasts, panties and bodies bumping to Taj's music. It was almost a relief when the house DJ returned to give everyone a break before Tiesto.

"Give 'em a minute to mop up the dance floor!" Taj joked. He held up his hand for a high five but the house DJ sidestepped him.

Taj shrugged, knowing just how hard it was to follow such a monster set. He made his way off the stage and across the dance floor as women everywhere pulled themselves together. Even the hostess Samantha looked dazed as she tugged her midriff shirt back into place and tried to smile. "Great, uh, set," she said sheepishly.

Taj would have smiled but the VIP booth was empty. "Hey, have you seen my friends?" he asked.

Samantha smoothed down her tousled blonde hair as she looked around. Her cute nose crinkled as she struggled to regain her composure and her blurry memory. "Um, I'm not sure, sorry."

Taj squinted toward a glowing exit sign, hoping to see his friends standing under it, but Skyler D and Phatty weren't there. "What the hell? They left?"

When he turned around Samantha was leaving too. She called over her shoulder. "Just getting you some fresh ice!"

Alone, Taj scooted into the enormous booth and checked his phone. He saw a message from Phatty. "We left, sorry, bro."

He tossed his phone onto the table and picked up an oversized bottle of expensive vodka.

Taj swigged from the bottle and then spoke to it. "I brought them to Vegas and they left my show without me? Fuck them, that's the last time I do anything for those assholes! Let the haters hate!"

He probably would have continued his one-sided conversation with the vodka bottle if Lance hadn't walked up to the table. Beside him was a very tanned man wearing a pink V-neck shirt and a shiny gold medallion. Taj swigged more vodka as the overly tanned man swept back his shoulder-length hair and smiled.

"Wow, Taj. That was one of the best sets I've ever seen," Lance exclaimed. "Great job up there!"

Taj tipped the vodka bottle one more time, but the alcohol sloshed out too quickly and dribbled all down his chin. "Thanks, Lance. I couldn't have done it without you." Then he wiped his mouth and smiled. "Or maybe I could have."

Lance ignored Taj's messy cockiness and turned to the man in the pink shirt. "By the way, I'd like to introduce you to Jean. Jean is a promoter from Europe."

Jean leaned into the booth, gold medallion swinging, and gave Taj a kiss on each cheek and then a surprise peck right on the mouth. "Taj, that set was magnificent!"

Taj wiped his mouth. "Yeah, thanks."

"I need you in Ibiza!" Jean declared. "Will you come to DJ? There's a big show coming up!"

The vodka bottle sloshed again, but this time Taj didn't bother to mop up his messy chin. "Did you say Ibiza?"

"Yes, yes, you need to come to Ibiza and DJ!" Jean laid a hand on Taj's skinny shoulder.

"I know it is last minute, but please, will you come? I pay 100,000 euros, plus all expenses!"

"No way!" Taj looked at Lance, who nodded that the deal was real. "I've always wanted to go to Ibiza. They really know how to get turnt up out there!"

Lance stepped in before Taj and Jean could shake hands. "Make it 150,000 euros and you've got yourself a deal."

Jean laughed and swept back his long brown hair again. "This guy likes to bargain! Okay, I will do it."

The three men got all tangled up trying to shake each other's hands. Taj was so excited he jumped out of the booth, vodka bottle still in hand. Lance stopped him before he hugged Jean.

"I'll set up the arrangements and get the contract drawn up right away," he said.

"Alright!" Taj shot his fist into the air and did a quick spin move.

Jean was just as excited. He rubbed his hands together and said, "This will be a big show. Big! Over 10,000 people!"

He got a hold of Taj again and kissed first his cheeks and then his lips before spotting someone else he knew and trotted away. Lance caught Taj wiping away the kiss and they both laughed.

"Dude! 150,000 euros? Ibiza, Spain? 10,000 people? This is the best night of my entire life! Wait until I tell my dad."

Lance patted Taj's shoulder. "You're the man, Taj. Your parents will be so proud. I'll make sure your flight is booked for tomorrow night. Now go and get some rest!"

When Lance was gone, Taj flopped back into the big, empty booth. He grabbed the half-empty vodka bottle and dumped some of the liquid into a glass when the headliner appeared in front of him.

Tiesto grinned. "Taj, that was epic! Those were some dope beats you were playing. The energy was crazy!"

"Tiesto!" Taj exclaimed as he jumped up. He was so excited he blurted out the big-time DJ's name at a deafening volume before gaining control of his voice.

"Hell yeah, I mean, thanks, man! I've been a fan of your music for a long time."

"Right on," Tiesto said. "Keep up the good work. You're going places!"

Taj pointed at Tiesto with both hands. "Gotta learn from the best to be the best!"

He was about to invite his hero to party with him when he remembered the DJ's set was about to start. The crowd had recovered and was buzzing back to the dance floor. Taj looked to see if Skyler D and Phatty were somehow in the crowd, but they weren't there.

"I'll see you around, man," Tiesto said. "Take care."

"For sure! Catch you later! Hey, Tiesto, maybe next time I'll be headlining and you'll be opening up for me!" Taj chuckled as he sat down.

The headliner lifted an eyebrow as Taj swigged from the bottle again. "What a jackass," Tiesto said, and then he walked away.

Taj continued to celebrate even though he had to do it solo. It didn't take long for the vodka to hit him hard, and soon he was stumbling through the casino, trying to dance.

He'd lost one shoe and his laptop bag was slipping dangerously off his shoulder. Taj had his beats playing through his headphones and kept up a steady string of self-compliments. "Who's the man? I'm the man. Taj is the man. I'm the best DJ in the world!"

Taj hiccupped violently down a row of slot machines. He pumped his fist in the air with a spaghetti-limp arm as he yelled, "Woohoo!"

At the elevator, Taj's double vision aligned long enough for him to recognize a familiar face. It was Nicky, the raunchy storyteller he met before his rise to stardom. She was about to duck away and run, but when he stepped closer, she caught the sound of his music blaring out of the headphones around his neck.

Her eyes lit up and she licked her glossy lips. "Hi, Taj. Like, what a surprise! Do you remember me? We met at that lounge a while back."

Taj hiccupped so hard he sounded like a stepped-on frog, but that didn't deter Nicky from wrapping her arms around his neck. "Yeah, I remember you. Long time no see! What are you—"

Before he could finish his sentence, Nicky stuck her tongue down his throat. The kiss was more of an assault, but Taj didn't mind at all. He jammed a drunken finger into the elevator button and hung on to Nicky as he swayed.

"Going up to your room?" Nicky asked. She bit his bottom lip and grinned. "Me too."

In the elevator, Taj tried to slip his hand down Nicky's pants but got his fingers caught in her pocket. They were still tangled together when the doors opened and they stumbled down the hallway to Taj's suite.

One look at the luxurious accommodations and Nicky ripped off all her clothes. She tossed them around with wild abandon as Taj blasted his music through the suite's high-end speakers.

Nicky gyrated and swayed her naked body back to where she'd flung her purse and pulled out a bag of capsules.

"Wanna get freaky? Let's take some Molly," she giggled.

"Yeah, I'm down! Where is she?" The room was spinning but Taj didn't care.

Then Nicky shimmied in front of him and bent over. Ass in the air, she inserted one capsule into the abyss and then looked over her shoulder expectantly.

"Go ahead," she purred. "Take your medicine."

Taj swayed, then dropped to his knees and leaned in. What did he care what Skyler D and Phatty were up to? He'd show them how a real star partied.

CHAPTER SEVENTEEN

DIRTY DEEDS

Skyler D stepped out of his small shared room wearing a new shirt he couldn't afford. Instead of high rolling in Vegas, he should have been at home booking himself more gigs.

That thought reminded him of the screaming fans that had flooded the dance floor for Taj last night.

Skyler D swore. "Lucky bastard."

He shut the hotel room door softly so as not to wake up Phatty and turned down the hallway. He was determined to win big somewhere in the casino and show Taj how Vegas was really done.

Then he noticed the door to Taj's suite was open. Skyler D should have kept going, he was mad enough at his friend to ignore him completely, but curiosity made him pause and peek inside.

Taj was sprawled out across the suite floor on top of a messy nest of cushions, blankets and what looked like a damp assortment of hotel towels. It was early enough that no one else was in the hallway, so he slipped inside the open door.

Taj's snoring punctuated in a loud snort and Skyler D froze. Then, still dead asleep, Taj cooed, "Yeah, girl, you wanna hear my beats?"

"Amateur," Skyler D muttered.

He spied Taj's laptop open at the end of the suite's elegant bar. He had to pick his way through room-service trays and half-empty bottles of booze and wipe away a handful of strip club flyers before he could tap the keyboard.

The laptop lit up with a screensaver shot of Taj's family. He proceeded to scan the desktop and found a folder titled "My Beats" and opened it to find hundreds of files. He had just clicked on the trashcan icon when Taj woke up.

"Um, hey, bro. Uh, what are you doing?" Taj asked.

Skyler D slammed Taj's laptop closed and tried to smile. "Well, just, um, I just needed to use your computer for a sec."

Taj heaved himself up to a sitting position and then struggled to his feet. He gripped his head and asked, "Why the hell did you and Phatty leave last night?"

Instead of answering, Skyler D knocked over a pair of vodka bottles and pretended it was an accident. "Sorry, bro," he said.

Taj pried his eyes open and looked around the suite as if just remembering where he was. "Wait. How'd you get in here? Where's Nicky?"

"Nicky?" Skyler D laughed. "Oh, man, please tell me you didn't."

"Seriously, man." Taj rubbed his forehead. "When'd you break into my suite?"

"I didn't break in. The door was wide open." Skyler D started to march indignantly toward the door but had to pause when he got closer to Taj. "Hey, when did you grow a mustache?"

Taj's eyes widened as he remembered. "Nicky," was all he could say.

Skyler D leaned closer to study Taj's upper lip. "And what is that smell, dude?"

"Never mind!" Taj grabbed a towel from the floor and wiped his face furiously. "You can use my laptop if you want."

Taj grabbed his computer and held it out to his friend.

Skyler D started to distract him with Dirty Sanchez stories, but it was too late. Taj saw his beats folder open side by side with the trashcan.

"What the...? Were you gonna delete all my tracks?" Taj asked.

Skyler D refused to make eye contact even when Taj stepped closer. "What the fuck, bro? I thought you were my boy!"

Skyler D bit his lip, but he couldn't hold back his pent-up anger anymore. "Fuck you, Taj. Fuck you! I'm supposed to be doing the big gigs. I should be bagging all the bitches. I'm supposed to be where you're at. You've only been DJing for a year!"

"What?" Taj put down his laptop and slumped against the suite's private bar. "You can't be serious. You're supposed to be happy for me, dude."

"Happy that you stole all the shine from me?" Skyler D shouted. "You're here because of me! None of this would be happening if it wasn't for me giving you another shot to DJ! You should be thanking me!"

Phatty peeked in the door. "Everything okay?"

"Fuck you, Skyler!" Taj was exploding. "That's the most selfish shit I've ever heard. Ever since I started making music, everyone except my mom and Phatty has given me a hard time.

"I'm finally getting some love from people and one of my best friends turns out to be a jealous prick!" Taj closed up his laptop and made a big show of tucking it safely in his bag.

"I was your best friend," Skyler D snarled. "Now I'm outta here!"

Phatty had to dive into the suite and flatten himself against the wall so Skyler D wouldn't knock him over as he stormed out.

"Dude, what happened?" Phatty asked Taj.

Taj's hangover was gone, but the lingering effects of betrayal felt worse. "Fuck you too, Phatty! Where'd you go last night? The hostess told me you guys left."

"Dude, I was—"

Taj picked up the silver lid to the ice bucket and winged it at Phatty. "Whatever, bro! I don't want to hear it. Just leave with Skyler. I'm done with the two of you!"

Tears welled up in Phatty's eyes and he was too speechless to even open his mouth. Without a word, he turned and left Taj's suite, considerately closing the door quietly behind him.

Taj stood dumbfounded in the wreckage of his hotel suite. He wanted to be defiant, to show them he didn't need anybody, but suddenly Las Vegas felt big and empty.

Taj clenched his jaw and tried to be determined, but he

didn't have the heart to pull his laptop back out and get to work. Instead, he tucked it into the bottom of his suitcase.

Taj continued to pack for Ibiza in silence; he didn't even have the desire to listen to his own music. As he was gathering up the last of his belongings and rolling them into a ball, he heard his phone buzz.

"Apologizing already," Taj snickered.

Taj's face lit up when he checked the phone. The text message was not from Phatty or Skyler D.

Janet had texted: "Hi, stranger. Looks like you made a good impression in Vegas!"

Taj grinned over the clapping-hands emoticon and flopped onto his king-sized hotel bed to text back. "Hi, Janet! Sorry I haven't had a chance to reach out much. I thought of you last night during my set!

"It was one for the history books. I just got booked to perform in Ibiza and I leave tonight. Wish you could come!"

The reply was almost instant. "Wow, that's so exciting! I'm so jealous! I've seen videos on the internet of the parties out there. Looks lit! Don't worry, I'll be there in spirit :)."

Taj paced around the room, not sure how to broach the subject that was really on his mind, so he texted: "This is my first time DJing overseas and my first time traveling alone. So, how's the new boyfriend?"

He had to wait a painful twenty seconds until Janet replied. "Well, have fun out there! It's nothing serious. LOL. Let's link up when you get back. :)"

"Yes!" Taj jumped off his bed and danced around in

a circle before texting: "For sure, I'm down. It's about time. I think we have a lot in common."

"You're too sweet. I do too! But you can have any girl on the planet and I'm nothing special."

"Stop that, you got it going on!" Taj spoke out loud as he typed the message.

Janet responded instantly. "Yeah, but you don't even know me really. LOL."

Taj couldn't keep the smile off his face. "I can tell by your Instagram we make a good match."

"Is that right? Well, I look forward to getting to know you better. Enjoy your trip and be safe! I'll be waiting for you."

Taj pressed his phone to his heart before quickly texting: "You better! Thanks, gorgeous."

He waited a full two minutes just in case Janet responded, and then Taj texted his father. "Hi, Dad. Just got booked to perform in Ibiza. I'm leaving Vegas today and heading straight to Spain."

Taj was all done packing by the time his father managed to text back. "Proud of you, son. Be safe."

"How's Mom?" Taj texted.

The response came so fast that Prasad must have already been typing it. "Your mother is not feeling well. We'll talk about it when you get back."

That last sentence worried Taj, but it couldn't over-shadow the fact that he had actually received some praise from his father.

After the fight with his friends, even those few words made Taj feel better. He was about to text back and ask more about his mother when he received an actual phone call, this one from his agent.

"Hey, Lance. I'm all done packing!" Taj said.

"Great, great. I'm just calling because Jean left money for your expenses. He wanted to make sure you have everything you need, including a nice wardrobe for Ibiza."

"Nice!" Taj was pumped as he looked down at his rumpled outfit in sudden disgust.

Lance continued. "Before you head to the airport, why don't you stop by a few of the hotel stores and pick out some stuff."

"You got it, Lance. I'll go get laced up!"

The first place that Taj headed was the Rolex store, where he was easily convinced he needed a $20,000 limited-edition watch from the Oyster Perpetual collection. Then he strutted over to the Versace store where the security guard hesitated but finally let him in.

Taj smiled at the stoic man and turned on his headphones.

Instantly, two shop girls flew over to help him. "I like the look of those jeans, ladies. How about you help me try them on?"

The girls loosened the buttons of their shirts and bustled him into a fitting room.

When he finally reappeared, Taj wore lipstick kisses on both cheeks, diamond-encrusted sunglasses, a bright-white V-neck shirt and bright-purple jeans.

He strutted to the counter. "I'll take 'em!"

The Versace employee nodded his head, having seen it all. "Fabulous. I love those jeans. My sister has the exact same pair."

Taj choked a little. He had no choice but to wear the women's jeans like he was making a statement. It didn't matter as long as he turned up his hottest new tracks.

CHAPTER EIGHTEEN

MILE-HIGH CLUB

Taj's confidence was back as his stretch limo pulled up to the airport curb. He flipped a fifty-cent casino chip to the airline employee that greeted him.

The man ignored Taj's "tip" completely and picked up his luggage without a word. Taj strutted through the automated doors.

"Goodbye, Vegas. Try not to miss me too much." Taj turned to blow a kiss over his shoulder, bumped into the airline employee, and got checked by his own suitcase.

He stumbled into an arriving flux of tourists and was almost swept back out to the curb. The airline employee shook his head and led the way to the first-class ticket line.

Taj was glad when his luggage had been checked in and he was free to walk to the security line by himself. "That guy was totally ruining my vibe," he assured himself out loud.

He clicked on his speaker backpack and adjusted his music to a low hum. The effect was immediate: three female flight attendants that had just rushed into the doors behind him suddenly slowed. He smiled at them each in turn and winked at the last one.

All three women stopped completely, not caring if they missed their flight, as they gazed at Taj.

Smiling to himself, Taj sauntered into the shortest line and laid his still-playing backpack and laptop bag on the conveyor belt.

He danced to his own beats as he emptied his pockets and dumped everything into the airport security bin.

The nearest TSA agent, a burly man with a sour look of perpetual stomach pains, spotted Taj's purple jeans. His only response to Taj's smile was a curt gesture. "Next."

The metal detector immediately lit up and the TSA agent gave a heavy sigh. "Sir, did you empty everything from your pockets?"

Taj patted his pockets with sweaty palms. "Yeah, they're empty."

"Ok. I'm going to need you to walk through the detector once more," said the annoyed TSA agent.

"Sure, no problem," said Taj nervously.

The metal detector beeped loudly as soon as Taj inched forward, and the TSA agent swallowed hard. He rubbed his stomach as he stepped out from behind the metal detector to herd Taj in a new direction. "Please come with me. We're going to have to do a full cavity search," the TSA agent said.

Taj suddenly couldn't blink. "Who is?" he asked.

"She is," the man said as he pointed to a wider-set female TSA agent.

Instead of her colleague's sour look, she had a tight, satisfied smile that made Taj's stomach flip.

He watched as she snapped a glove on one hand and turned her evil smile on him.

"Um, she's not really my type!" Taj yelped as he was handed over.

A torturous amount of time passed but Taj still managed to make his flight. He hobbled to his seat and eased himself into the plush first-class chair with a small whimper. There, he stretched and tried to tell himself the window view made up for his ordeal with TSA.

"Ibiza, here I come," he whispered with red, watery eyes.

After a bumpy takeoff that almost left him in tears, Taj was working on his laptop, headphones firmly on, when a brunette flight attendant stepped into the aisle. Her long legs and obviously nonregulation skirt had every male in the plane leaning in. She bent down, leaned into each row, and swung her hips up and down the aisle until she finally reached Taj.

"Hello, sir. Would you like a beverage?" she asked.

Taj's eyes were glued to a message from Janet and his music was pumping loudly through his headphones. The flight attendant leaned down low enough to cause the man across the aisle to pause from his lengthy novel and glance down at the woman, tilting his reading glasses to see better.

"Would you like a beverage?" Her soft hair swung into Taj's line of view as she tugged his headphones down around his neck.

"Sure. Can I have a water and two aspirin?" Taj asked.

She didn't move, and Taj was glad he hadn't missed the view. The brunette flight attendant's low-cut blouse beat out the passing Rockies with no contest. She pressed a little closer, licking her lips as she heard his music playing. Her eyes sparkled as Taj looked her up and down.

She whispered in his ear. "When the seatbelt sign turns off, meet me in the rear bathroom."

"YOLO!" Taj whispered excitedly. "I mean, I'll meet you there."

As soon as the pilot stopped yammering on about clear skies and finally switched off the seatbelt sign with a loud *bing,* Taj wiped off his sweating hands and stood up. He somehow managed to unbutton half of his shirt despite getting tangled in his headphone cords as he navigated the narrow airplane aisle. He checked that his beats were still playing, just loud enough to be heard close up, and then popped open the bathroom door.

The flight attendant wasn't there yet so Taj stepped inside and left it unlocked.

He was prematurely congratulating himself on joining the Mile-High Club when there was a loud knock on the bathroom door.

"Mmm, I like when they aren't shy," Taj said, but he yelped when the bathroom door was ripped open.

An obese woman three times Taj's size took up the entire door opening. There was nowhere to run. She put one beefy foot into the bathroom before she even noticed Taj and then it was too late.

She heard his music and her chubby cheeks bunched into a big smile. He struggled to turn the music off, but accidentally pressed the repeat button. "Noooo!" Taj shrieked.

Two nuns seated near the bathroom heard the commotion, made the sign of the cross and put their headphones on.

"Come to Momma!" She squeezed into the small bathroom with a hungry look in her eyes and then closed the door.

The plane bounced up and down for a brief second, triggering the seatbelt sign to flash.

Five minutes later she forced her way back out of the narrow door and shoved her way down the aisle to some unfortunate row in economy.

Taj emerged a minute later looking even more rumpled. His forehead throbbed as he wondered over and over again exactly what folds of copious skin the woman had actually pressed against him. At his seat, he practically dropped himself down, and took a quick selfie.

It assured him he didn't look quite as bad as he felt, so he posted it on Instagram with the hashtag: #airplanesickness.

Janet immediately commented with a picture of a thermometer, followed by, "Feel better!"

"Thanks," Taj commented after a series of grateful emojis. "Can't wait to chill soon."

Just the idea of sitting with Janet, even if it was on the sofa in his parents' living room, was so relaxing that he was finally able to tip his head back and fall asleep. Exhausted, he fell into a deep sleep and the airplane seemed far away as he started to dream.

A heavy jungle surrounded him, and Taj tried to wish himself back to the comfortable plushness of his first-class seat, but the dream wouldn't let him. He had no choice but to push his way through the thick jungle leaves until he stumbled into a clearing.

There was the same tent he had dreamt of before, puffs of white smoke billowing out the top, the flap door folded open.

"No thanks," Taj said, but he found himself entering the dream tent despite his wishes.

The flap closed and hit him on the backside as he tripped into the tent.

The same yogi in a pristine white robe sat in the center, a small fire at his folded feet.

Taj didn't even try to replicate the man's intertwined lotus prayer position but knelt down stiffly in front of him.

"Hello? Heeeelllllooooo?" Taj called.

Thin tendrils of incense smoke slipped across his vision as he studied the mysterious old man, but Taj couldn't make out if he was familiar or not. Though, the frequency of the soft sitar music that surrounded them matched Taj's beats. He could feel it in his bones.

"Who are you?" he muttered.

Taj had just leaned closer to examine the old man when his eyes flew open. "I've been expecting you," he said.

"You have?"

The yogi smiled and looked deep into Taj's eyes. "Do you know why you are here?"

"I don't even know where I am!" Taj exclaimed.

The yogi shook back his long white sleeves and pointed to a spot on the ground directly in front of Taj. "You are here."

"What is all this?" Taj asked.

"You are here because you have been tampering with the sacred sounds of the Earth, and you must stop." The yogi did not blink as he spoke, his eyes locked on Taj.

"What do you mean?" Taj asked. The dream was so vivid the incense smoke made his nose itch.

"You have been forewarned, Taj. If you continue, your karma will suffer greatly!"

A shadow fell over the dream as Taj became genuinely scared. "I can't stop now. I'm finally a superstar! This is all I've ever wanted!"

"I urge you to stop, Taj. Now, be gone from this sacred space." The yogi vanished.

Taj woke up to the airplane pilot announcing their impending arrival. "Hi, folks, this is your captain speaking. We are now beginning our descent for Ibiza Airport."

Taj pressed his nose to the small airplane window. The island still looked tiny from his vantage point, but the ocean was bright blue. He studied the amazing landscape until the guru's words came back to him.

"What did he mean? Sacred sounds of the Earth?"

Taj's confused muttering was cut off by the captain again.

"Ladies and gentlemen, please put your seats in the upright position and buckle your safety belts. We will be landing shortly." His short announcement was followed by the bright *ding* of the seatbelt sign.

Taj braced himself, but it was a smooth landing, and soon he was slipping on his sunglasses and exiting the airport into the bright Spanish sun.

CHAPTER NINETEEN

IBIZA OR BUST

S quinting despite his dark shades, Taj finally spotted a man standing in front of a black stretch limo with a small plated sign that had his name on it.

"Welcome to Ibiza, Mr. Das. I'm Angelo, your driver." The man tipped his small cap and took Taj's suitcase. "Jean instructed me to drive you directly to the venue."

Taj smiled, sure everything would go smoothly from there on out, then he missed the curb and stumbled hard against the limo's sleek paint job. His bag banged against the babied car and the driver gasped. Then Taj saw his laptop fall. It slipped from his bag and tumbled over as Taj scrambled to catch it.

Everything was in slow motion as the laptop fell to the concrete and three large pieces broke completely off the ruined computer.

"Noooooooo…" changed to "ffffuuuuuucccck!" Taj collapsed onto his knees next to his shattered laptop.

"What the hell am I going to do now!? I'm fucked!"

The limo driver was busy buffing the side of the car with his sleeve. "Is everything alright, sir?"

"No! I am so fucked!" Taj cried. He crawled into the limo with his arms wrapped around the remains of his computer. The driver shrugged and shut the door after him, checking the paint job one more time before he headed to the driver's seat.

Taj pried open his laptop and pressed shaky fingers to the cracked screen. He pleaded and prayed as he turned it on, but the screen remained black. In a panic, Taj pressed both hands to the sides of his face.

Angelo tapped on the brakes and sent the broken laptop skipping across the limo floor. "Sorry for the delay, sir. This is the only way to the venue and tonight is the beginning of the biggest festival on the island."

"Or the end of my career," Taj whimpered under his breath.

He crossed his fingers and silently hoped the traffic stayed bumper to bumper long enough for a miracle to save him. Taj almost bumped his head against the limo ceiling when his phone jangled an incoming message.

It was from Janet: "Have an amazing show! :)"

"Oh god, oh god, oh god," Taj muttered as he typed a quick "Thanks."

By the time the limo pulled into the venue, the sun had already set. With the natural lightshow over, the crowd was pressing toward the stage and ready for the music. The promoter, Jean, grabbed the limo door handle before the car had stopped.

"C'mon, c'mon, Taj, you're late!" Jean clutched his arm and propelled him toward the stage.

Taj scrambled to escape him. "I know but my laptop, all my music..."

Jean pushed harder. "The crowd is massive! There's thousands of people waiting for you! Nice pants. Very you."

Taj's new clothes felt too tight and were suddenly drenched in cold sweat. "Maybe I should change?" he squeaked.

Jean shook his head and ushered Taj through the club. The thick crowd parted just enough to snap photos. Even with all the flashes blotting his vision, Taj could see he was in the most exquisite outdoor club he had ever seen. His feet turned to cement as he realized he was not only out of his depth but Taj was completely alone and without anything or anyone to save him.

The house music pulsating from the speakers had become an ominous ringing noise in Taj's ear as Jean nudged him along the stage to the steps. Two steps up, Taj made the mistake of turning around and looking at the crowd.

It was a warm night and everyone was dressed to show off their bronze tans. In comparison, Taj looked pale as dust, as if he'd just crawled out from underneath a rock.

"I feel sick," he whined to Jean.

"Good, good, we'll talk more later!" The promoter blocked the bottom of the stairs and gestured for Taj to make his big entrance.

The stage rose up at the center of the club with cabinets of speakers stacked as high as the eye could see. Off to one side was a lit pool with a gentle waterfall. The most beautiful women, vacationing from all over the world, lounged around the shallows in the smallest threads of bikinis. Supremely attractive bartenders served flashy and exotic cocktails and statuesque beauties skimmed through the crowd with exclusive bottle service.

Taj's mind reeled back to the Playboy Bunny leaping out of her own Lamborghini and running away from him. Then his complete flop of a performance at the Pearl came back to him like an elbow to the esophagus. He choked and coughed and could clearly hear Skyler D's voice in his head.

You need a gimmick…!

Then Prasad stood over his dizzy son.

Taj, I'm giving you one year to get your act together or else you're out of here…!

Taj snapped out of his awful daydream just as the house DJ finished up his set.

"You're on!" Jean hissed from the bottom of the steps.

When Taj didn't move, the promoter skipped up the steps two at a time and clamped on to his arm. "Don't fuck this up, Taj. There are a lot of important people here," Jean said in a panic.

He propelled Taj onto the stage as the crowd cheered. Taj hesitantly inched toward the DJ equipment as Jean took hold of the microphone himself.

"All you beautiful people! Just arriving from Las Vegas, I have the pleasure of introducing the sexiest DJ himself, Taj!"

Jean easily whipped the over-capacity crowd into a frenzy. Taj set down his laptop and opened it quickly, half expecting a miracle to have already happened.

The cracked screen remained black, and all Taj could do was take a deep breath. The crowd was chanting his name as beads of sweat formed at his hairline. Taj blinked against the perspiration dripping down his forehead and ran over to grab the microphone from Jean in a last-minute attempt to stall.

"Wow, Ibiza, you really know how to party! I'm excited to be here!" Taj cried.

The crowd went wild, but after a few more attempts at banter, it was obvious their energy was waning into confusion and irritation. Pockets of the crowd began to boo and ladies pouted and shook their pretty heads. In a panic, Taj started beatboxing. The boos grew louder and became angrier.

Jean looked from the crowd to Taj.

"What the fuck, Taj? Play something!"

Taj covered the microphone with one hand and shouted over the boos to the promoter. "That's what I was trying to tell you when I got out of the limo. I tripped and my computer fell on the ground."

"Use the other DJ's equipment! It's fine. Do something now!" Jean took a step back from the restless crowd and reminded Taj, "I paid you lots of money to come here."

The crowd surged forward. The loud boos had turned into angry shouts. Ibiza did not like to have their buzz broken up by technical difficulties or excuses of any kind. They shook their fists at Taj and demanded to be entertained.

Some people in the crowd laughed when Taj got overwhelmed. He ran off the stage right past Jean, holding up his laptop as if it were a shield. "Where do you think you're going, Taj!?" Jean screamed.

Most of the crowd hoped it was all part of the show until Taj reached the doors and escaped the nightclub.

He sprinted out into the street and spun around wildly.

His limo driver, Angelo, looked up from buffing the sleek black car and pushed his hat back on his head. Taj charged toward him, sweating profusely.

"Get the fuck back here!" Jean shrieked. "You son of a bitch! You'll never step foot in Ibiza again!"

Terrified, Taj didn't dare to look back. "Please, take me to the hotel!" he cried to the limo driver.

Angelo saw the nightclub doors pop open and the angry crowd flood out. He could see beer bottles clenched in their fists and was immediately afraid for his perfect paint job.

"Right away, sir!" Angelo chirped.

He whipped open the limo door and Taj leaped inside. They sped away as the first bottles started breaking on the road behind them.

CHAPTER TWENTY

HUMBLED BY THE FUMBLE

The next day, Taj finally pried his face off his tear-soaked pillow. He wished the hotel was on an entirely different island, but he was still stuck in Ibiza. The thought of showing his face, even to get to the airport, made him press the pillow back over his head.

The soft darkness insulated Taj, but he still heard his phone beep. He groped across the hotel bed, grabbed his phone, and finally peeked out from the puffy pillow.

Taj assumed it was Skyler D or at least Phatty, but his friends hadn't even liked his social media posts for days. Their silence blurred his vision with a whole new wave of tears. He'd failed far away from home and no one even cared where he was.

Except for Lance.

Taj winced and opened the email entitled "Gallery." He was surprised the subject line was not expletive-laden. Feeling shaky but hopeful, Taj sat up and read the email out loud: "Taj, I booked you to perform at an intimate art gallery event next Friday night in L.A. There will be some very big spenders attending. Something different from DJing in the club, but it pays $10,000."

Taj paused to whistle at that number, then he gulped as the email continued. "On another note, I got a message from Jean demanding his money back. He says you freaked out in Ibiza and ran off the stage? Fuckin' A, Taj! That's not good for your reputation or mine! We'll have to meet when you get back to discuss everything. I'm not happy to hear about this."

The phone clattered out of Taj's hand and fell to the hotel floor. He flopped down and reached for his pillow just as his phone beeped again.

He tried to convince himself not to check it. There was no chance it would be either of his friends after how he left things in Vegas, and Taj was too depressed to reach out. Still, the urge to hope and check his messages was too strong, and Taj finally grabbed his phone.

"Hey, how was your performance? :)" Janet texted.

Taj laid back on his hotel bed, his eyes finally clearing as he typed back to her: "I blew it! :(I dropped my laptop and it shattered. I couldn't play any of my beats and the promoter wants all his money back."

There was barely a pause before Janet texted back. "Oh no! I'm so sorry. Wish I could be there to make you feel better. :)"

"Yeah, me too," Taj typed. "My life is over. I'm flying out of here today! Hopefully I don't get recognized at the airport."

"Don't worry, that wasn't your last show," she wrote back.

"It could be. Once people in the states find out what happened! Hopefully no one posts anything or blogs about it. I'm so bummed."

Janet sent a row of bottles and bubbles. "People were probably so drunk they don't even remember."

Taj sat up and smiled. "Thanks for making me feel better. You're so sweet. It means a lot, but I still don't know what to do now."

She didn't hesitate to help with another text. "We all have our ups and downs. You can never give up at what you love doing! Even the best of us have off nights."

Taj pulled himself off the hotel bed and started throwing stuff in his suitcase. He knew he could make it to the airport if he just kept his eyes on Janet's sweet texts.

All packed, he stopped to text her again. "I just need time to reflect. Hey, btw, you like art, right?"

"Definitely! Why?"

Taj grinned, looking to the future. "I'm DJing at this art gallery Friday night. Wanna meet up there?"

Her response was instant. "Finally! LOL. I'd love to. :) Just send me the address and time."

Taj was so excited he could barely text: "Cool, it's a date!"

"Hope you can make time for me while you're DJing. ;)"

Suddenly, Taj remembered his old external hard drive. Now all he had to do was get home and make sure he didn't screw up again.

"I'll make time. No excuses," Taj promised Janet.

He forced himself downstairs and into the lobby. Angelo had refused to drive him anymore for fear of his beautiful limo getting scratched. Taj stepped outside, wondering where to get a cab. He was just starting to feel awful again when a video message popped up.

Taj watched Janet smiling and waving. He took a deep breath and walked to the beach. It didn't matter if he was recognized, Janet deserved a view of the gorgeous beach. He captured a seagull riding the soft breezes and the waves softly scrubbing across the beach. Then he ended with a shot of tourists doing yoga.

"Great way to relax before a flight!" Janet texted with a thumbs-up.

"She's right," Taj decided, and stumbled across the warm sand to join the group.

He kicked off his flip-flops, tossed down his suitcase and tried to stretch himself into Downward Dog. He took a deep breath and finally felt a little peace.

"This is your last chance!" The yogi appeared on the ground between Taj's legs, his white robe bright against the sand.

"What the—?" Taj fumbled forward and his face dug into the sand.

When he sat up, the guru was nowhere in sight. He glanced around the beach again but saw nothing unusual except an eagle soaring far overhead.

"Man, I gotta make some changes," Taj finally admitted.

Taj arrived home at dawn. Exhaustion blanketed his face as he staggered through the front door. He noticed a light was on in the kitchen. He lightly set his luggage down and walked softly toward the kitchen trying to avoid waking anyone. As he entered, Taj was surprised to see his mother standing there, stirring a cup of hot tea.

"Mom, you're up early."

As Aashi slowly looked up to see Taj, joy lit her face. She put her mug down and smiled at him.

"Hi, Taj, I'm so happy to see you!"

"Me too, Mom." Taj rushed over to give Aashi a gentle embrace.

"So, how are you feeling?" he asked with concern. "I talked with Dad a few days ago and he said you weren't doing well."

Aashi's hand caressed the side of Taj's face. "Come sit with me, my son."

Taj took a seat with Aashi. A bottle of prescription medication and a bundle of flowers in a vase were on the table. Aashi reached for the medication bottle.

"What is that?" Taj asked.

Aashi looked at her son. "Well, I didn't want to worry you because you've been on the go and doing so well with your career. Your music is great, and you bring joy to people when you play it, don't ever forget that."

Taj's eyes began to tear up. He reached for Aashi's hand and held it. "So, what did your doctor say?"

Aashi looked at the note on the flowers, and then at Taj. "Well, he said my cough is due to tuberculosis, but it's curable as long as I act fast. I have to go for treatment and stay on this medication for a few months. But I'm already feeling a little better."

Taj sighed in relief. He held his mom's hand tighter. "Mom, you're the strongest woman I know. And I'm here for you. We're going to beat this together!"

Gentle tears came down Aashi's cheek. "I love you, Taj." She sniffled. "Yes, we are. I believe in the power of positive thinking and I'm healing myself as we speak."

"That's the spirit!" Taj cheered. "You got this!"

They hugged again.

"Oh, before I forget to tell you," Aashi said, "I saw Phatty at the store yesterday. He looked very depressed. Is everything alright with him?"

Taj dropped his shoulders and looked down at the floor. "Not really. I got upset at him during our Vegas trip and insulted him pretty badly. We haven't spoken since."

Aashi gently lifted Taj's face by his chin and replied, "Maybe you should call him and say hello. You know life is so short, and he's like a brother to you."

Taj nodded his head and smiled. "You're absolutely right."

Aashi smiled back. "You look hungry, let me make you something."

"Thanks, Mom. I'm gonna go call Phatty first."

Taj walked upstairs to his bedroom, pulling out his phone as he went. He called Phatty.

Not far away, Phatty ignored his phone and focused on the same video game he'd been playing since getting back from Vegas.

He hadn't shaved in a week, his face mottled with dark stubble that didn't quite make up a beard. His bedroom was cluttered with fast-food bags, soda cans and spilled candy. He grabbed a few pieces off his bedspread and popped them into his mouth as he adjusted his headset and got back to the video game.

Taj called again. Then again.

Phatty sighed and tried to ignore him, but his eyes fell on an old photograph. Skyler D and Taj probably didn't remember the day it was taken, but they were all little kids and stood with skinny arms wrapped around each other's shoulders.

"Fuck, not now!" Phatty whined. He adjusted his headset again and called out, "Squad leader, I need backup. Come in, squad leader!"

"You're on your own, soldier," came the terse reply.

Phatty gritted his teeth, but it was too late. His avatar had stood still two seconds too long and got killed. He watched himself get shot and die.

"Dammit, squad leader! You son of a bitch! Where's the leadership?" Phatty yelled.

The prepubescent voice squeaked, "Screw you, dipshit!"

"Fucking ten-year-old," Phatty snapped. He ripped off his headset and grabbed his phone. "Yo."

"Phatty? Hi!" Taj said.

"What up, Taj," Phatty replied coldly.

Taj was excited and talked too fast. "Hey, bro, just got back from Ibiza last night."

Phatty rolled his eyes and ate another handful of candy. "Yeah? How was it?"

There was a long pause, strange coming from Taj. "So, let's just say it wasn't one of my best sets."

"What happened? Was it a train wreck?" Phatty sounded hopeful.

"Yeah, pretty much. I'll tell you about it next time I see you." Taj paused again and took a deep breath. "Yo, dude, I'm calling to apologize about Vegas. I don't know what got into me. I guess all this fame and success really made me lose sight of who's been there for me from the start, you know? I'm really sorry about everything."

"You are?" Phatty asked around a mouthful of gummy bears.

"Yeah. I didn't even hear you out that day."

Phatty grunted. "Yeah, you were a total douche, but

then I found out Skyler tried to trash your beats, so I totally understand. I would've been pissed too."

Taj let out a huge sigh.

"Thanks for understanding!"

"I wanted to stay at your show that night in Vegas, but Skyler was being bitchy and forced me to leave. You were killing it, bro!"

"You're the only true friend I have left," Taj said.

"Of course, dude! I'm happy for you. Maybe one day when I get as popular as you, you'll remember all this and agree to be my roadie for free."

Taj laughed. "Anytime! Yo, by the way, if you're free Friday night, you should come check out this art gallery. I'm DJing."

Phatty looked around his wreck of a bedroom and turned off his TV. "Yeah, I should be free that night. I could use a break."

"Cool! I'm gonna need your help, if that's okay. I'll fill you in on Friday." He held his breath in case Phatty was still mad at him.

Phatty was not. He smiled. "Cool. Right on. I'll see you Friday."

Taj hung up his phone with a smile, but it slipped as soon as he heard a knock on the door. "Come in," he sighed.

Prasad walked into his messy bedroom. "So, how was your trip?"

Taj tried to be strong, but his father was very happy to see him and genuinely interested about his big show. His shoulders slumped as he admitted, "It was terrible, Dad! My laptop broke and my beats wouldn't play. I got booed off stage. It was so humiliating."

Prasad put a hand on his son's shoulder and squeezed.

"I'm sorry, son. Would it help if we got you a new laptop?"

Taj looked up and blinked in confusion. "What?"

His father squeezed his shoulder again. "I finally realize how much this music means to you and how far you've come with it. If this is what you truly love, I want you to be happy."

"You do?" Taj asked.

Prasad sighed at his son's disbelief. He spoke slowly. "I began to realize I was projecting my own fear of chasing my dreams onto you. That fear came from my own father discouraging me all the time. Your mother helped me understand I was making the same mistakes with you." With his eyes tearing up, Prasad took a deep breath. "Taj, I support you and your dream."

Taj leapt up and surprised his father with a tight hug.

Then both men pushed back and found it much easier to talk about new laptops.

CHAPTER TWENTY-ONE

TRUTH IN ART

The art gallery featured a large collection of sacred geometrical art. The sleek, white walls were hung with enormous interlocking pieces, individual works that created sanctified equations and small personal examples from the artist's trial and error.

Bright track lighting illuminated each piece, and small silver placards explained the complicated geometry.

Taj felt very out of place.

Everywhere in the wide white room, admirers nodded and understood the esoteric art.

He guesstimated a few hundred people strolled through the gallery, and every one of them understood the messages more than him.

All the men looked successful in clean, pressed blazers. The women wore formal dresses that whispered across the spotless gallery floor. Twanging, experimental music filled the room but could not drown out the curator's carrying voice as he described the artwork as fresh, already classic and sure to complete anyone's art collection—as long as they had deep pockets.

In the far right corner, a table draped in matte black offered free drinks and hors d'oeuvres. Opposite that, Taj stood at another black-draped table and worried people would mistake him for a waiter despite the turntables and speakers.

Taj shuffled in his signature Crocs and held his head-phones to his ear in order to maintain his perfectly spiked black hair. He figured he could pretend to be busy mixing beats if anyone asked him to refresh their drink.

"Yo, yo, yo!" called Phatty.

Taj's friend had dressed up for the occasion in a light-blue button-up, khaki pants and dress shoes. There was a ketchup stain on Phatty's collar that ruined the whole ensemble, but Taj was glad to see him. He reached out and their high-five slap reverberated through the gallery.

"Hey, bro, glad you made it! It's good to see you, man," Taj said. He flagged down a real waiter and made sure his friend got a handful of crudités.

Phatty took a bite of one and smiled. "Good to see you too. Wow, I really like the art in here. Definitely digging the vibe. And all these beautiful ladies! Thanks for the invite."

Taj nervously tapped at his laptop as Phatty finished up his handful of snacks. "I'm just glad you came."

"Need any help setting up?" Phatty asked.

"Just about done. Think I'm all set." Taj looked up from his laptop and grinned. "I'll need your help behind the tables a little later, though."

"Seriously?" Phatty stopped looking for the next tray-carrying waiter and turned back to Taj.

"Yeah. Are you down to spin a few tracks? I'm meeting this girl here," Taj said.

Phatty spotted a pretty girl in a tight dress as he nodded. "Sure, I get it. No problem!"

He gestured with a thumbs-up and promptly forgot about the girl as another waiter walked by with a tray of stuffed mushrooms. He grabbed a handful, plus some of the garnishes, then spun gracefully to grab a glass of wine from another tray. The girl in the tight dress got distracted from the art and watched with an arched eyebrow as Phatty chowed down.

"Hi! I'm with the DJ," Phatty said with his mouth full.

She was not impressed, and walked away.

"Speaking of," Taj said. He cleared his throat and picked up the microphone. After a shriek of feedback, he had everyone's attention. "Hi, everybody, I'm Taj and I'm going to play some music for you all tonight. Now, let's get the vibe right!"

Taj pressed play on his new laptop and tapped his toe as the baseline pumped out of the gallery speakers. A few of the art pieces rattled as the music got going.

Seconds later, women were turning away from the geometric shapes, their eyes focusing on the DJ. The sophisticated women licked their lips and let their hips swing as they drew closer and closer to Taj.

He scanned the beautiful and now receptive crowd but wasn't wowed until he caught sight of Janet. She appeared in the gallery door, her elegant violet dress like a vibrant flower in a sea of serious black gowns. Taj smiled, slack-jawed as he watched her walk past all the art pieces, her wavy brown hair bouncing as she nodded to the beat.

He was puzzled, and wondered why Janet wasn't responding to the music like the rest of the women.

"Phatty!" Taj called frantically to his friend as the increasingly turned-on women closed tightly around the DJ table.

"Excuse me, ladies. I'm with the DJ," Phatty said, but he still had to shove to fit through the crowd.

He only stopped when he came shoulder to shoulder with a lovely blonde woman at least a foot taller than him. "Whoa. An Amazonian!"

"C'mon!" Taj hissed.

Phatty winked at the tall woman who didn't see him at all. "So, what's the plan, Taj?" he asked.

"Okay, okay." Taj forced himself to take a deep breath that did not calm him down a bit. "Janet just got here."

"Dude, why isn't she coming over here?" Phatty asked.

"I know. I was wondering the same thing," Taj replied worriedly.

Phatty nudged Taj. "Bro, what if she's a he?"

Taj's eyes bulged at the possibility. "Phatty, I need you to take over and keep the music going while I find out what the deal is."

Phatty glanced at Taj's laptop screen and shrugged. "Okay, no problem."

Taj grinned at his friend and tossed him the headphones. "Just enjoy the ride!"

Taj dove under the black tablecloth and managed to scoot out just before the crowd trapped Phatty in completely.

Pleased with his escape, he paused to give Phatty a thumbs-up. His friend, overwhelmed by the enthusiastic response of the women, could do nothing but wave frantically.

Women were now close enough to claw at him and Phatty blushed furiously.

"Hey, ladies, be careful! This is my best shirt!"

Taj wondered for a second if he should go back and help his friend, but then he caught sight of Janet again. "Now's my chance!" Taj reminded himself.

Janet turned and saw Taj and his heart melted as a big smile spread across her beautiful face.

Taj tried to act cool, but a group of women shoved him out of the way. Janet giggled as Taj recovered, but soon the frenzy surrounding the DJ table got out of hand.

Taj took Janet's hand only to realize she had been pointing to the DJ table. "What? What's the matter?" he asked.

Phatty had embraced his newfound attractiveness and was dancing with a large group of women. A few hips hit the table and the music skipped. Then Taj saw the black tablecloth flip up.

"Oh, no," he groaned.

A pair of fallacious women licked their lips and crawled under the DJ table, preparing to surprise Phatty when he turned around. Unfortunately, the buckles of one woman's scrappy heels caught on the surge protector. In her excitement, she yanked the plug from the wall.

The music stopped.

"Oh, shit. Not cool!" Phatty cried into the now dead microphone.

The two women scrambled out from under the DJ table with horrified looks. All the dancers stopped and looked at each other in confusion.

"Oh shit, oh shit, oh shit!" Phatty scrambled to figure out why the music stopped.

"Please, no!" Taj was sure his chance with Janet was over. His plan had fallen apart. Now he had to force himself to turn around and look at her again.

Taj was stunned. Instead of seeing confused rejection, Janet was still smiling. Then she waved and her friend Linda appeared, tousled from her wild dancing near the DJ table.

Linda immediately waved and then switched to sign language. "Hi, Janet! What are you doing here?" Linda signed.

Janet smiled shyly and glanced over to Taj. "Not now, Linda. Just give me a few minutes," Janet signed.

Linda gave Taj a skeptical look but nodded. She signed, "Okay, sorry!"

A pretty pink blush touched Janet's cheeks as she turned back to Taj. Her voice was soft and slightly fuzzy. "Sorry I never told you I was deaf. I read lips really well."

Taj, astounded by the sign language exchange, shook himself and grabbed Janet's hand. "Hey, don't be sorry. It's no big deal!"

Janet ignored the clammy feel of his hand and held on tight. "I should have told you."

Taj's head spun, and he didn't know if it was the deafening silence of the gallery, the way Janet smiled, or the flood of memories he now knew he'd misinterpreted.

He could still see what Janet looked like the first night they met in the Pearl Nightclub.

It had been crowded and the people all around them had been loud and pushy. Taj remembered he had felt stupid trying to ask her "What's up?" and he had first thought it was a miracle that Janet had responded. Not only had a beautiful girl looked him directly in the eye, but she had smiled.

"What?" Janet had asked, her eyes on his lips.

Taj had scrambled to save her phone and then used his

own version of sign language, perfected on the loud dance floors of many clubs, to ask her, "Got a number?"

Janet was one in a million. Most girls pretended to be deaf when Taj talked to them in the nightclub. Janet had not only looked at him but answered his question!

He remembered how his heart had gone into overdrive as she had taken his phone and typed her number in.

He only remembered one little sign: her angry friend tugging on Janet's sleeve to get her attention. Taj had thought it was just rude, but now he knew why it took a physical touch to get Janet's attention.

She'd been smiling at Taj too much to even notice her friend until she felt her.

"Do you forgive me?" Janet asked in her fuzzy voice. Taj lifted her hand in both of his and kissed it.

He remembered how they had texted back and forth and he had asked, "Yo, what's your Instagram? I'll follow you back!"

Janet had replied, "It's @SweetJanet_86. BTW, I've been playing that beat you emailed me over and over. I love the bass!"

Taj had always wondered why Janet had mentioned the bass. She had never said anything about how the music made her feel because the special frequency had been lost on her.

Janet had truly liked Taj for who he was.

"Forgive you?" Taj snapped out of his memories and back to the murmuring crowd at the art gallery. "There's nothing to forgive!"

Janet smiled and knotted her fingers through Taj's. "Shouldn't you be up there?"

Taj looked back at the DJ table just as Phatty popped up from underneath the black tablecloth. He'd plugged the surge protector back in but lost the middle button on his shirt in the process. Phatty looked at it in despair as he hit play.

Who would want him with his hairy stomach sticking out? The music started up again and all the women cheered.

Phatty blushed again, a huge smile on his face, as the women ignored his protruding belly and fought each other just to touch him.

Taj watched Janet cautiously for a moment, but the sexy magic of the frequency still did not touch her. Janet happily danced and only had eyes for Taj. His head spun again, but this time he turned it into his best dance move.

Janet laughed and they both stopped dancing to have their first kiss.

Over her shoulder, DJ Phatty gave his friend the thumbs-up before disappearing once again into a sea of eager women.

CHAPTER TWENTY-TWO
A HAPPY ENDING

A month went by and everything seemed to be changing. Taj finally realized that the frequency was dangerous and decided to take it off of his beats. He told Janet all about it and even confessed to his hallucinations of the yogi.

Janet thought it was all a nice fairy tale, but even she could not deny the effect his music had on women.

"Yeah, everyone but me," she said playfully.

"Some women just have naturally better taste than others," Taj joked.

Taj was no longer wearing Crocs; Janet had thrown them away and bought him a pair of Dunks. He still wore his Members Only jacket, but now it had a heart-shaped patch on the inside pocket that Janet had embroidered.

Taj was headlining at the Pearl Nightclub again, but

this time there were no doubts from anyone. Lance had not disowned him despite the cost of the Ibiza failure and together, with the help of DJ Phatty standing in on nights Taj couldn't make it, his name was back in good standing.

As Taj stepped onto the stage, he blew a kiss to Janet and then grabbed the mic. At first his voice wouldn't come out. Everyone that had ever supported Taj was there, including his parents. Prasad looked up proudly at his son with Aashi at his side, and the feeling of accomplishment nearly overtook him.

Taj wished he could freeze the moment, because he realized for the first time in his life he was truly happy.

"Um, thank you everyone for coming out!" Taj finally squeaked. He cleared his throat and continued. "I couldn't have done this without your support. I love you all!"

The security guards held back the shrieking women as they reached out to touch Taj. He smiled at them, took a deep breath and continued.

"You all have given me more than you'll ever know. As a token of my appreciation, go to my website and download my new mix!"

The crowd cheered as Taj dropped the first beat of his set. He signaled to Janet to come onto the stage and celebrate with him. As she got close, he reached out for her hand and gently pulled her in. He whispered in her ear, but she couldn't hear it.

They collided with a long, passionate kiss.

63222519R00109